## "You don't want to hear why I've come?"

"I am certain I do not."

"That will make it fast, then."

Amelia could admit she felt...too much. Perhaps a touch of shame for having to come to Teo like this—especially after the last time she'd shown up here, uninvited. Her pulse kicked at her, making her feel...fluttery. And she was, embarrassingly, as molten and soft as if he'd smiled at her the way he had in September.

When he hadn't ventured anywhere near a smile.

*Just do it, be done with it and go*, she ordered herself.

And who cared if her throat was dry enough to start its own fire?

"I'm pregnant," she announced into the intimidatingly, exultantly blue-blooded room. To a man who was all of that and more. "You're the father. And before you tell me that's impossible, I was at the Masquerade last fall, and yes, I dyed my hair red."

## One Night With Consequences

*When one night...leads to pregnancy!*

When succumbing to a night of unbridled desire, it's impossible to think past the morning after!

But with the sheets barely settled, that little blue line appears on the pregnancy test, and it doesn't take long to realize that one night of white-hot passion has turned into a lifetime of consequences!

Only one question remains:

How do you tell a man you've just met that you're about to share more than just his bed?

Find out in:

*The Argentinian's Baby of Scandal*
by Sharon Kendrick

*His Cinderella's One-Night Heir* by Lynne Graham

*The Sicilian's Surprise Love-Child* by Carol Marinelli

*Bound by Their Nine-Month Scandal* by Dani Collins

*The Queen's Baby Scandal* by Maisey Yates

Look for more One Night With Consequences stories coming soon!

# Caitlin Crews

---

## SECRETS OF HIS
## FORBIDDEN CINDERELLA

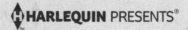

Recycling programs
for this product may
not exist in your area.

ISBN-13: 978-1-335-89333-8

Secrets of His Forbidden Cinderella

First North American publication 2019

Copyright © 2019 by Caitlin Crews

**Printed in U.S.A.**

www.Harlequin.com

*USA TODAY* bestselling and RITA® Award–nominated author **Caitlin Crews** loves writing romance. She teaches her favorite romance novels in creative-writing classes at places like UCLA Extension's prestigious Writers' Program, where she finally gets to utilize the MA and PhD in English literature she received from the University of York in England. She currently lives in the Pacific Northwest with her very own hero and too many pets. Visit her at caitlincrews.com.

### Books by Caitlin Crews

### Harlequin Presents

*Conveniently Wed!*

*Imprisoned by the Greek's Ring*
*My Bought Virgin Wife*

*One Night With Consequences*

*A Baby to Bind His Bride*

*Secret Heirs of Billionaires*

*Unwrapping the Innocent's Secret*

*Bound to the Desert King*

*Sheikh's Secret Love-Child*

*Stolen Brides*

*The Bride's Baby of Shame*

*The Combe Family Scandals*

*The Italian's Twin Consequences*
*Untamed Billionaire's Innocent Bride*
*His Two Royal Secrets*

Visit the Author Profile page
at Harlequin.com for more titles.

# CHAPTER ONE

"HIS EXCELLENCY IS not at home, madam." The butler sniffed, visibly appalled.

He did not so much bar the door to the grand and ancient palatial home as inhabit it, because such a glorious door—crafted by the hands of long-dead masters and gifted to the aristocratic occupants likely on bended knee and with the intercession of a heavenly host, because that was how things happened here in this fairy tale of a place that had claimed this part of Spain for many centuries—could not be blocked by a single person, no matter how officious or aghast.

And the butler was both, in spades. "One does not *drop in* on the Nineteenth Duke of Marinceli, Most Excellent Grandee of Spain."

Amelia Ransom, considered excellent by her closest friends instead of an entire nation and with decidedly lowbrow peasant blood to prove it, made herself smile. Very much as if she hadn't, in fact, turned up at the door of a house so imposing that it was unofficially known as *el monstruo*—even by its occupants. "I know for a fact that the Duke is in."

An old acquaintance of hers still lived in one of the nearby villages—"nearby" meaning miles upon miles away because the Marinceli estate was itself so enormous—and had reported that the Duke's plane had been seen flying overhead two days ago. And that the flag with the Marinceli coat of arms had been raised over the house shortly thereafter, meaning the great man was in residence.

"You mistake my meaning," the butler replied, his deep, cavernous face set in lines of affront and indignation that should have made Amelia slink off in shame. And might have, had she been here for any reason at all but the one she'd come to share with Teo de Luz, her former stepbrother and the grandiose Duke in question. "His Excellency is most certainly not at home to you."

It was tempting to take that as the final word on the matter. Amelia would have been just as happy not to have to make this trip in the first place. It had been a gruesome redeye flight out of San Francisco to Paris, particularly in the unappealing seat that had been all she could get on short notice. The much shorter flight to Madrid had been fine, but then there was the drive out of the city and into the rolling hills where the de Luz family had been rooted deep for what might as well have been forever, at this point.

"I think you'll find he'll see me," Amelia said, with tremendous confidence brought on by fatigue. And possibly by fear of her reception—and not from the butler. She stared back at the man with his ruffled feathers and astonished air, who did not look convinced. "Really. Ask him."

"That is utterly out of the question," the butler retorted, in freezing tones. "I cannot fathom how you made it onto the property in the first place. Much less marched up to pound on the door like some…salesman."

He spat out that last word as if a salesman was akin to syphilis.

Only far more unsavory.

If only he knew the sort of news Amelia had come to impart. She imagined he would cross himself. Possibly spit on the ground. And she could sympathize.

She felt much the same way.

"I expect you go to great lengths to keep

the Duke's many would-be suitors from clamoring at the door," she said brightly, as if the butler had been kind and welcoming or open to conversation in any way. "He must be the most eligible man in the world by now."

She'd personally witnessed the commotion Teo caused when enterprising women got the scent of him, long before he'd assumed his title. That was why she hadn't even bothered attempting to get in the main gates, miles away from the front entrance of the stately home that was more properly a palace. The grand entrance and gates were guarded by officious security who could be reliably depended upon to let absolutely no one in. Amelia had therefore driven in on one of the forgotten little medieval lanes that snaked around from the farthest corner of the great estate, there for the use of the gamekeeper and his staff. Then she'd left her hired car near the lake that had been a favorite reading spot of hers back in the day.

That way she could walk to clear her head from the flight and so little sleep, prepare herself for the scene before her with Teo and best of all, actually make it to the soaring front door that would not have looked out of place on a cathedral. Her car would have been stopped. A woman on foot was less noticeable. That was her thinking.

She hadn't really thought past getting to the door, however, and she should have.

The butler was slipping a sleek smartphone from the pocket of his coat, no doubt to summon the security force to bodily remove her. Which would not suit her at all.

"I'm not another of Teo's many groupies," Amelia said, and something flashed in her at that. Because that wasn't *precisely* true, was it? Not after what she'd done. "I'm his stepsister."

The butler did not do anything so unrefined as *sneer* at her for the unpardonable sin of referring to Teo by not only his Christian name, but a nickname. He managed to look down his nose, however, as if the appendage was the highest summit in the Pyrenees.

"The Duke is not in possession of a stepsister, madam."

"Former stepsister," Amelia amended. "Though some bonds far exceed a single marriage, don't they?"

Her smile faded a bit as the butler stared down at her as if she was a talking rat. Or some other bit of vermin that didn't know its place.

"I doubt very much that His Excellency recognizes *bonds* of any description," the butler clipped out. His expression suggested Amelia had offended him, personally, by suggesting otherwise. "His familial connections tend toward the aristocratic if not outright royal and are all rather distant. They are recorded in every detail. And no *stepsisters* appear in any of these official records."

Amelia pressed her advantage, scant though it was. "But you don't know how Teo feels about members of the various blended families his father made while he was still alive and marrying, do you? Do you really dare send me away without finding out?"

And for a long moment, they only stared at each other. Each waiting to call the other's bluff.

Amelia wished that she'd stopped somewhere and freshened up. She'd dressed to impress precisely no one back in San Francisco many, many hours ago, and she was afraid that showed. She didn't particularly care if Teo saw her looking rumpled, but butlers in places like this tended to be far more snobbish than their exalted employers. Her ratty old peacoat was a good barrier against the blustery cold of the January day. The jeans she'd slept in on the long flight from San Francisco were a touch too faded and shoutily American, now that she considered it in the pale Spanish morning. And the boots that hadn't seemed to need a polish back home seemed desperately in need of one now, here on the gleaming marble stair that led inside the palatial house she still dreamed about, sometimes.

Because *el monstruo* was truly a fairytale castle, and then some. There were turrets and dramatic spires, wings sprouting off this way and that, with pristine land rolling off on all sides toward the undeveloped horizon. Standing here, it was easy to imagine that the breathlessly blue-blooded family that had lived here for the better part of European history was the only family that had ever existed, anywhere.

The de Luzes would no doubt agree.

Of all her mother's husbands—all the titled gentlemen, the courtiers with hints of royalty, the celebrities and the politicians who had found themselves charmed and captivated and discarded in turn by the notorious Marie French—none had impressed themselves on Amelia as much as Luis Calvo, the Eighteenth Duke of Marinceli. Teo's father, whom Marie had pursued, caught and then inevitably lost over the course of a few whirl-wind years when Amelia was still a teenager.

As formative experiences went, finding herself thrust into the middle of a world like the de Luzes', so excruciatingly exclusive, deeply moneyed and aristocratic that they might as well have lived on another planet altogether—and for all intents and purposes, did—had been as ruinous as it had been ex-hilarating. Marie had always preferred rich men. But add together every conventionally rich man in the world and it would still barely scratch the surface of the de Luz fortune. And the nineteen generations of power and influ-ence that infused it, expanded it and solidi-fied it.

Amelia had not recovered as quickly from this marriage as she had from the others her mother had subjected her to over the years. Or from this *place.* And most of all, she had never quite gotten over the man who lived here now, his father dead and gone. And when she'd belatedly performed a much-needed ex-orcism to get rid of the hold those years kept on her, she'd soon discovered that she'd cre-ated a far bigger problem.

*You've come here to create a solution,* she reminded herself primly.

Not that it would matter why she'd come if she couldn't get in the door.

Teo de Luz—once her forbidding, stern and usually outright hostile stepbrother, now the latest Duke in a line so long and storied she'd once heard giddy society types braying to each other that the de Luz family was, in fact, *Spain itself*—wasn't the sort of man who could be waylaid. There were no accidental meetings with him in local coffee shops; he owned half the coffee farms in Kenya. He did not frequent public gyms or lower himself to the questionable hospitality of bars or restaurants accessible to the hoi polloi. He had chauffeurs. Private jets. Shops closed to accommodate him, restaurants offered him their private rooms, and he stayed in secluded villas in the few locations where he did not hold property, never public hotels.

The sorts of places he went for fun didn't bother to put names on the doors. You either knew where they were, or you didn't. You were either in the club, or you were out.

If you had to ask, you didn't belong.

Amelia was sure that if she looked closely at the de Luz coat of arms, that's what it would read.

As the daughter of Marie French, Amelia had grown up *close to* a lot of money, but never *of* it. Her mother was famous for her many divorces, and she'd certainly gathered herself a tidy sum from various payouts—alimony, divorce settlements, baubles and properties that had been showered upon her by this lover or that—but the kind of wealth and power that the de Luz family had in spades and demonstrated so decidedly here wasn't the sort that could be amassed by one person. Or within one lifetime.

It would take twenty generations to even make a dent.

If Amelia could turn back the clock and make all of this go away, she would. If she could reach back these few, crucial months and slap some sense into herself long before she'd had her brilliant idea at the end of the summer, she'd swing hard. Her palms itched at the notion.

But wishing didn't change the facts.

"Please tell Teo that it's me," she said sunnily to the dour man towering over her, possibly prepared to stand right where he was for another twenty generations. She smiled as if he'd already agreed. "Amelia. His favorite stepsister."

She was fairly certain she was not Teo's

favorite anything, but that wasn't something she planned to share. And for another long, tense moment, there on the front step where she could feel the winter wind bite at her, Amelia thought that the butler would slam the door in her face and let the estate's security detail sort her out.

A part of her hoped he would. Because surely, if she'd gone to all the trouble to fly herself to Spain, turn up on his doorstep and *try* to tell him what she needed to tell him, that was enough. Above and beyond the call of duty, really.

She could only do so much, after all. It wasn't *her* fault the man chose to barricade himself away like this.

*He wasn't barricaded away last fall,* a voice inside her that she was terribly afraid was her conscience chimed in.

It had been late September when she'd found her way here last. She'd come under the cover of darkness, blending in with the extensive crowds who flocked to the estate for the Marinceli Masquerade that took place every fall to commemorate the birthday of the long-dead Tenth Duke. It was a glittering, diamond-edged fantasy that had been going on in one form or another for three hundred years. Amelia had come with such a different purpose then. It had been her one opportunity to enact her exorcism, and she had dedicated herself to the task. She had dressed like a stranger and had even gone so far as to dye her hair and wear colored contacts. Because she had her mother's violet eyes, and people did tend to remember them.

And she'd spent the months since congratulating herself on a job well done. Sometimes immersion therapy was the only way to go. Even when she'd understood what she'd inadvertently done, she hadn't regretted what she'd done—only what the result of it would ask of her.

But today, it was creeping toward midday, and the weather was raw. This part of Spain was covered in a brooding winter storm that had made her drive from Madrid dicey. Particularly when she'd skirted around the mountains—the snow-covered peaks of which she could feel, now, in the frigid wind that gusted at her as she waited for the butler's decision.

She didn't particularly relish repeating that drive, especially without getting what she'd come for here. But she would do it if necessary. And then she would hole up in a hotel somewhere and either try to come up with a new plan to find Teo and speak to him, or she would simply go back home and get on with this new life of hers.

She was giving herself a little pep talk about what that would look like when the butler stepped back, and inclined his head.

Very, very slightly. Grudgingly, even.

"If madam will wait here," he said, beckoning her inside to what she supposed was the foyer. Though it bore no resemblance to any other foyer Amelia had ever seen.

It always seemed to her like its own ballroom, dizzy with chandeliers, mosaic-worked mirrors and statuary clearly meant to intimidate. This was not a stately home built to offer invitations. Quite the opposite. It had been, variously, a fortress, stronghold, the seat of a revolution, a bolt-hole for a deposed king, the birthplace of a queen and a long list of other dramatic accomplishments that Amelia had spent two very long, very lonely winters studying. Right here in the vast library that soared up three floors, commanded its own wing and was more extensive than many university collections.

Amelia smiled at the butler, though she could admit it was mostly saccharine, as he shut the heavy door behind her.

He did not return the favor.

He indicated a stone bench against the wall and waited until Amelia sat.

"This is a private home, madam, not a museum," he intoned. At her. "It is certainly not open to spontaneous visits from the public. Please respect the Duke's wishes and stay right here. Do not move. Do not explore. Do you understand?"

"Of course," Amelia said, frowning slightly, as if wandering off into the house where she'd once lived had never occurred to her.

Then again, the last time she'd actually lived here had been ten years ago and she hadn't felt free to wander gaily about the place then, either. That she was unwelcome here had been made very clear. From Teo, certainly, if not from his distant father, who had been interested only in his scandalous new wife. And certainly from the legion of staff who were possessed of their own opinions about the notorious Marie French as their new mistress. Her teenage daughter had been, at best, a casualty of that war.

Or anyway, that was how Amelia had always felt.

And always stern, usually visibly horrified Teo, with those simmering black eyes, that blade of an aristocratic nose and that cruelly sensual mouth that haunted her dreams in ways that only made sense later—

Well. That had never helped.

The Amelia who had been so bent on exorcism would have launched herself into action even as the butler's footsteps faded away, echoing off into the maw of the great house that stood proud around her. That version of herself had been deeply committed to reclaiming her life. To making something she wanted out of the things she'd been given and the things that had been pressed upon her, one way or another.

She really had made huge changes in her life last summer. She had settled in San Francisco, for one thing. No longer did she travel about with her mother, forced to act in all kinds of roles that only put strain on their already unconventional relationship.

Her first attempt at setting healthy boundaries with Marie had come when Amelia had insisted on going to college, an enterprise that her mother had found amusing at best and actively baffling at worst.

"There's only one school that matters, silly girl," Marie had said, laughing wildly in that sultry way of hers that Amelia had watched pull men to her from across vast ballrooms. "We call it Hard Knocks University and guess what? Tuition's free."

Unlike many women who, like Marie, married and divorced with the pinpoint accuracy of an expert marksman, Marie had always delighted in the fact that she'd produced a child. But then, that was the thing the dismissive, disparaging tabloids had never understood about her. Was she a gold digger? Almost certainly. But she was also earthy, charming and frequently delightful. She collected husbands because she fell for them, spent their money because she only fell for wealthy ones and moved on when she was bored. She'd made it her life's work. And yet many of her discarded ex-lovers still chased after her, desperate for another taste.

Amelia never knew if she admired her mother or despaired of her.

"I don't think a life of ease, cushioned by alimony payments from some of the richest men alive, constitutes the school of hard knocks," Amelia had replied drily.

Marie had thrown up her hands. Literally. And Amelia had gotten her first taste of victory.

She had loved college. She had hidden away

in Boston for four wonderful years. She'd walked along the Charles. She'd spent lazy, pretty afternoons on the Common. She'd taken trips on the weekend down to the Cape or explored the out-of-the-way harbors that dotted the rocky Maine coast. She'd camped in the Berkshires. She'd hiked through the turning leaves in the New England fall, gotten maple syrup straight from the tap in Vermont and had stayed in stark farmhouses that reminded her of Edith Wharton novels.

She had studied anthropology. Sociology. Poetry. Whatever took her fancy as well as the finance and business courses that gave her a solid foundation to best serve her mother's needs. And for four glorious years, she'd been nothing more and nothing less than another college student in one of the best college towns in existence.

After graduation, she'd gone straight back to the job she'd been preparing for all her life. Her mother's personal assistant, financial manager, moving specialist and far-too-often on-call therapist.

It was that last part that got old, and fast. Last June, Amelia had decided that she was never going to live her own life if she was too busy parsing every detail of Marie's. That was when she'd decided that of all the places she'd been, she could most see herself living in beautiful San Francisco.

"But I almost never go to San Francisco," Marie had protested. And she'd laughed when Amelia only stared back at her blandly. "Fair enough."

Her summer in San Francisco had felt like the life Amelia had always wanted. She was twenty-six years old. The perfect age, or so it seemed to her, to be on her own in a marvelous, magical city. She could handle her mother's affairs from afar, and did, and only rarely had to fly off to sort out whatever disaster her mother had created across the world somewhere.

Amelia had even decided that she might as well start dating. Because that was what normal people did, according to her friends. They did something other than marry in haste, then repent in the presence of swathes of legal teams, the better to iron out advantageous financial settlements.

But a funny thing happened every time Amelia had tried to lose herself in the moment and let passion—or a third glass of wine—sweep her away. Not that there was much *sweeping*. If she let a date kiss her, and even if she enjoyed it, the same thing happened every time.

Sooner or later, instead of getting excited about her date, she would find herself imagining simmering black eyes. That impossible blade of a nose that gave him the haughty look of an ancient coin—ones that were likely made from the piles of gold the de Luz family hoarded.

And that stern, sensual mouth that could only be Teo's.

Damn him.

The terrible truth she'd discovered last summer was that she couldn't seem to get past her once-upon-a-time stepbrother. And she might not have thought of the Masquerade, but she'd been in Europe anyway. Marie had summoned Amelia to attend to her as she'd exited one love affair and started another in Italy. And somehow, while moving Marie's things from one jaw-dropping Amalfi Coast villa to another, Amelia had started thinking about the Marinceli Masquerade at *el monstruo*. Filled with people in the September night, all of them draped in masks and costumes as they danced away the last of summer the way they'd been doing for generations.

Surely it was the perfect opportunity to get that man, her former stepbrother who took up too much space in her head, out of her system. Once and for all. Because Amelia felt certain that in order to have that normal life she wanted, she really might like to do more than kiss a man someday.

That meant she was going to have to *contend with* Teo.

And once the notion had taken hold, Amelia couldn't seem to think about anything else.

But then, the funny thing about life was that there were always so many different and unexpected ways to repent a moment of haste. Her childhood had taught her that. Her mother was the poster girl for repenting over the course of years and through lawsuits, some brought against her by the angry heirs of men who had attempted to win her favor via excessive bequests.

In Amelia's case, it wasn't a single moment she needed to repent. More like a stolen, astonishing hour.

As soon as she could breathe again, she'd crept out one of the many side doors in this monstrosity of a private palace. She had fled under cover of darkness and she had never meant to return.

Therefore, naturally, here she was. A little more than three months later, sitting on a hard stone bench surrounded by grimacing old statues that glared down at her in judgment. As if they knew exactly what she'd done and resented her for her temerity.

"You and me both," she muttered at them.

And regretted it when her voice seemed to roll out before her, tumbling deep into the quiet depths of the house.

Of course, the historic seat of the Marinceli empire wasn't simply *quiet*. It was self-consciously, dramatically *hushed*. Not the sort of sound that came from emptiness or neglect, but was instead one more marker of impossible wealth. Wealth, consequence and a power so deep and so vast it stretched back centuries and more to the point, infused the very stones in the ceilings and the walls.

If a person really listened, they could *hear* all that might and glory in the lush quiet, even sitting still in the foyer, as directed.

Amelia unbuttoned her coat, letting the heavier flaps fall to her sides. She'd learned a long time ago that there was no point competing in places or situations like this. She was always so obviously and irrevocably American, for one thing. That she would therefore be considered gauche and inappropriate by a certain set of Europeans was understood. And no matter what she wore or how she comported herself, or even if she adopted excruciatingly correct manners, she would always be seen through the lens of her mother. So she'd learned long time ago that she might as well stop trying to convince anyone otherwise.

Things that couldn't be changed, Amelia had found, could often be fashioned into weapons.

From far off, she heard the sounds of approaching footsteps, and braced herself. She held her breath—

But it was only the butler again. He appeared before her, gazing at her with suspicion, as if he expected to find her cutting the paintings out of their frames and stuffing them down the back of her jeans. Amelia smiled. Widely.

If anything, that seemed to horrify him more. She could tell by the way his chin seemed to recede into his neck.

"If you will follow me," he said, every syllable dripping with disapproval. "The Duke is a very important man. He is excessively busy. You will do well to bear in mind the compliment it is that he has chosen to carve out a few moments to entertain this untoward and wholly discourteous appearance of yours."

"I'll be sure to thank him," Amelia said, rising to her feet. The butler only stared back at her. "Profusely."

But the added word didn't seem to help. The butler turned on his heel and stalked off. Amelia followed, impressed against her will at the sheer umbrage he managed to carry in his shoulders.

He led her through the great hall, then off into the long gallery that connected the main part of the house to some of its seemingly haphazard wings. It was thick with portraits of black-eyed, haughty-looking men in a variety of historical outfits. She had been in the same gallery before, as an obsessed sixteen-year-old, tracking the evolution of Teo's features through ages and ancestors.

Today she found it wasn't Teo's features she was thinking of, or not entirely. She was trying to imagine all these fierce old aristocrats combined with her, and coming away with nothing much besides a wholly unwelcome stab of guilt. She did her best to swallow that down as they left the gallery and moved farther into the labyrinth of the grand house.

All the rooms they passed were the same.

Everything gleamed, a beacon of understated, exceptional taste. There were no knickknacks. No personal items. No shoes kicked beneath a couch or empty mugs on a table. Each room was arranged around a color scheme, or a view, or some other unifying notion. There were no antiques in the general sense. If she recalled correctly, every item in this house was priceless. Literally without price because any value attached would be too exorbitant. The house was filled with hand-selected, finely wrought pieces of art that had been presented to the family at one point or another by grateful, obsequious artisans and vassals and would-be allies.

The butler stopped, eventually, with the click of his heels and tilt of his head—both of which he managed to make an insult— before a door. Calculating quickly, Amelia figured that this must be the Duke's study. Ten years ago, Teo's father had spent his days here, conducting his business when he was at home. She'd had absolutely no occasion to venture to this part of the house, and after an initial introductory tour, hadn't.

It was only now, as the butler opened the door and ushered her inside, that she acknowledged the flutter in her belly. Not only acknowledged it, but accepted that she couldn't quite tell if it was anticipation, fear or a spicy little mix of both.

The door closed behind her with a quiet click that she felt was as passive-aggressive as the rest. But she had other things to think about.

Because this room, like every other room in this palace, exuded magnificence, wealth and quiet elegance. It was its own little library, and "little" only in comparison with the grand one across the house. There was a fire in the hearth and gleaming bookshelves packed tight with books—and not in matching volumes, with gold-lettered spines, suggesting no one touched them. This was a working library. A personal collection, clearly. There were even photographs in frames on the shelves, almost as if a regular human lived here and collected memories as well as priceless objects. There was a surprising amount of light coming in from the winter day outside, through the glass dome atop the ceiling and more, through the glass doors that opened up over the gardens.

Amelia took all of that in, and then, slowly and carefully—as if it might hurt her, because she was terribly afraid it might—she let her eyes rest on the man who waited there. He leaned against the vast expanse of a very old, very beautiful antique desk that somehow managed to connote brooding masculinity and centuries of power in its lines.

Or maybe that was the man himself.

He was like a song that sang in her, that called the dawn, that changed the world.

Teo de Luz, once upon a time her stepbrother and now a far greater problem in her life, waited there as if he was one of the statues she'd seen in the hallways, crafted by old masters with decidedly famous and inspired hands. And this was not one of the few, very rare photographs of him that a person could find if they deep-dived online. This was not the man she'd found at the Masquerade last September—masked, hidden and diluted in some way, she'd assured herself, even if his touch had not felt *diluted* in any way. This was not even the stepbrother she remembered from ten years ago.

Teo was older now. He was beautiful and he was ferocious, and it was truly awful, how a single man could seem as imposing and great as the ancient house they stood in.

And suddenly, Amelia was all too aware of every choice she'd made that had brought her here to stand before him. She felt as fatigued and threadbare as her jeans.

She ordered herself to speak, but when she lifted her chin to do so, she found herself… caught.

Because even here, in his own private library with the weak winter light pouring in and a fire crackling in a fireplace—all things which should have made this scene domestic and soft—Teo was something *more* than merely a man.

He was always bigger than she remembered. Taller, more solid. His shoulders were wide and the rest of him was long, lean, and she knew, now, that he was made entirely of muscle. Everywhere. His black eyes simmered, like his ancestors' out there in the long gallery, but she had somehow dimmed the effect of them in her mind. In person, he was electric. His hair was still inky black, close cropped, and she saw no hint of gray at his temples. He had those unfair cheekbones that might have seemed pretty were it not for the masculine heft of his nose, and then, below, that sensuous, impossible mouth that made her feel flushed.

Especially because now she knew what he could do with it.

And she hadn't seen him clearly that night in September. That had been the point. She had been bold and daring, and he had responded with that brooding, overwhelming passion that had literally swept her off her feet. Into his arms, against a wall. And then, in a private salon, still dressed in their finery, with fabric pushed aside in haste and need.

Too much haste and need, it turned out.

Even though she had watched him roll on protection.

But now, he wore nothing to cover his face. And he wasn't smiling slightly, the way he had then. Those dark eyes of his weren't lit up with that particular knowing gleam that had turned her molten and soft.

On the contrary, his look was frigid. Stern and disapproving.

It made her remember—too late, always too late—that he wasn't simply a man. He was all the men who had come before him, too. He was the Duke, and the weight of that made him…colossal.

A decade ago, on the very rare occasions that he had looked at her at all, he had looked at her like this.

But it felt a lot worse now.

"This is a surprise," Teo said, with no preamble. "Not a pleasant one."

One of his inky brows rose, a gesture that he must have inherited from the royal branch of his family tree, because it made Amelia want to genuflect. She did not.

"Hi, Teo," she replied.

Foolishly.

"You will have to remind me of your name," he said, and there was a gleam in his eyes now. It made her feel quivery in a completely different way. And she didn't believe for a second that he didn't know who she was. "I'm afraid that I did not retain the particulars of my father's regrettable romantic choices."

"I understand. I had to block out a whole lot of my mother's marriages, too."

A muscle worked in his lean, perfect jaw. "Allow me to offer a warning now, before this goes any further. If you have come here in some misguided attempt to extort money from me based upon an association I forgot before it ended, you will be disappointed. And as I cannot think of any other reason why you should intrude upon my privacy, I will have to ask you to leave."

Amelia considered him. "You could have had the butler say that, surely."

"I will admit to a morbid sense of curiosity." His gaze swept over her. "And it is satisfied." He didn't wave a languid hand like a sulky monarch and still, he dismissed her. "You may go."

Amelia ordered the part of her that wanted to obey him, automatically, to settle down. "You don't want to hear why I've come?"

"I am certain I do not."

"That will make it fast, then."

Amelia could admit she felt...too much. Perhaps a touch of shame for having to come to him like this—especially after the last time she'd shown up here, uninvited. Her pulse kicked at her, making her feel...*fluttery*. And she was, embarrassingly, as molten and soft as if he'd smiled at her the way he had in September.

When he hadn't ventured anywhere near a smile.

"Never draw out the ugly things," Marie had always told her. "The quicker you get them over with, the more you can think about the good parts instead."

*Just do it, be done with it and go,* she ordered herself.

And who cared if her throat was dry enough to start its own fire?

"I'm pregnant," she announced into the intimidatingly, exultantly blue-blooded room. To a man who was all of that and more. "You're the father. And before you tell me that's impossible, I was at the Masquerade last fall and yes, I dyed my hair red."

She could only describe the look on his face as a storm, so she hurried on.

"And because you asked, I'm Amelia Ransom. You really were my stepbrother way back when. I hope that doesn't make this awkward."

# CHAPTER TWO

HIS EXCELLENCY MATEO ENRIQUE ARMANDO
DE LUZ, Nineteenth Duke of Marinceli, Grandee of Spain, and a man without peer—by
definition and inclination alike—did not
care for American women in general or the
loathsome, avaricious Marie French in particular. He had viewed her corruption of his
once proud father as a personal betrayal, and
had celebrated their inevitable divorce as if it
were his own narrow escape from the grasping woman's mercenary clutches.

That his father had fallen for such a creature had been a deep humiliation Teo was terribly afraid stained him, too. They were de
Luzes. They were not meant to topple before
such crassness, much less *marry* it.

His father's subsequent wives had, at the
very least, been from a certain swathe of European aristocracy. Only Marie Force had

managed to tempt the Eighteenth Duke into breaking from centuries of tradition. Only her, a coarse and common woman whose gold digging had already been a thing of legend.

Teo was the only heir to dukedom that had never been polluted in living memory—until Marie.

By extension, Teo had never cared for Marie's daughter, either, with those same unearthly purple eyes that had always seemed to him a commentary on her character. Or decided lack thereof.

Even though Amelia had been little more than a child—*sixteen is not precisely a toddler,* came a contrary voice inside him that he chose to ignore—Teo had been certain her sins had been stamped upon her then, every new curve a bit of dark foreshadowing. With such a mother, she had only ever been destined to head in one direction.

"Pregnant," he said, as if tasting the word.

"Coming up on eighteen weeks," she replied, with rather appalling cheer. When he only gazed at her in disbelief, she continued. "If you count backward, you'll find that it matches right up with the Masquerade."

"Thank you, Miss Ransom," Teo replied after a moment, in the frigid tones that usually made those around him quail, scrape and apologize. The woman standing just inside the door of his study looked notably unaffected. "I am capable of performing simple mathematical equations."

All she did was smile. As if she doubted him, but was magnanimously keeping that opinion to herself.

It…irritated him. And Teo was rarely irritated by anything—because his life was arranged to avoid anything and anyone who might dare to annoy him in any way.

Perhaps he should have expected something like this. Pregnancy claims upon him were always and forever naked attempts to grab a chunk of the de Luz fortune and then bask in the glory of the many titles, honors and estates that went along with the name. It wasn't really a surprise that this impertinent, insolent creature of questionable parentage had developed ideas above her station when she'd spent those mercifully brief years thrust into the exalted realm of his family.

Teo understood it, on some level. Who wouldn't wish to be a de Luz?

Amelia Ransom, still cursed with those indecorous purple eyes, stood before him on a rug so old that its actual provenance was still hotly contested by the historians who periodically combed through the de Luz house and grounds and wrote operatic scholarly dissertations on the significance of the family collections. That she should be deeply shamed by her presence here—and the fact that the carpet beneath her feet boasted a pedigree while she did not—seemed not to have occurred to her.

Especially while she was issuing preposterous accusations. Involving fancy dress and dyed hair, of all things.

It was all so preposterous, in fact, that Teo could hardly rouse himself to reply further.

Because he was the current head of one of the most ancient houses in the world, and the favor of his time and good temper was not granted to any bedraggled creature who happened along and turned up at his door.

Not that many creatures, bedraggled or otherwise, usually dared "turn up" in his presence. Or managed to "happen along" in the first place even if they did dare, as he employed what he'd believed until now to be an excellent security service. He made a mental note to replace them. Before the next dawn.

And remembered as he did that Amelia's mother had been notable chiefly for the things she'd dared. All of which she'd gone ahead and executed without the faintest notion of her own gaucheness.

Hadn't he always known that her daughter would turn out just like her?

"I've learned many things since September," said the creature before him. He had recognized her on sight, of course, though he had not intended to gift her with that knowledge. Because she should have assumed that she was entirely unworthy of his notice and his memory alike. Instead, she was talking at him in that same offensively *friendly* voice that made him think of overly bright, manic toothpaste commercials. "One of them— which you would think ought to go without saying—is don't disguise yourself and have relations with your former stepbrother and think there won't be repercussions."

"I have yet to accept that any 'relations' occurred," Teo said in what he thought was a mild voice, all things considered.

"Acceptance, or the lack of it, doesn't change the facts," Amelia replied, and Teo saw a glimpse of something steely in those garish eyes of hers. "And the fact is, I'm pregnant with your baby."

"How convenient for you."

He watched her from his position against his desk, where he felt significantly less at his ease than he had moments before. Amelia, meanwhile, did not seem particularly thrown by his reaction. There were no tears. No wilting or wailing, the way there normally was during outlandish pregnancy claims—if the reports he'd received were to be believed. If anything, she brightened.

"I'm informing you because it's the right thing to do," she told him, with a hint of self-righteous piety about her, then. "Not because I need or want you to do anything. Consider yourself informed."

She turned then, and Teo almost let her go. Purely to see if she would do what he thought she meant to do, which was march straight off—but only so far, as it was difficult to extort money from a man once ejected from his presence. He assumed she knew it.

He decided he wouldn't play her game. "Surely the point of disguising yourself, as you claim you did, and then deciding to have 'relations' with me under false pretenses, would be to stay. Not to flounce off because I've failed to respond as you would like."

It would have been easy enough to find photos of the Masquerade, he told himself. He had danced with a luscious redhead, then disappeared with her for a time. Anyone might have guessed what they'd been up to.

That certainly didn't mean that *this* woman was that redhead. His mind reeled away from that possibility even as his body readied itself, remembering.

Amelia waved a distinctly impolite hand in the air, and compounded the disrespect when she didn't turn back to face him. "I don't care what you do with the information, Teo. I think we can all agree that it's appropriate to inform a man of his paternal rights. That's all I wanted to do, it's done, the end."

"Surely a letter would have sufficed."

She did turn then. Not all the way. She looked back over her shoulder, and he was struck against his will.

Hard.

Teo truly hadn't believed that Amelia Ransom, of all possible people, was the mysterious woman he'd enjoyed so thoroughly at the Masquerade last fall. But he remembered… this. Almost exactly. The hair had been a bright red, the eyes a dramatic shade of green that now, in retrospect, he should have known was false, and she'd worn an intricate mask that took over the better part of her face. The mask had been a steam punk design and so intricate, in fact, that she'd claimed she couldn't remove it—and he hadn't cared, because her mouth had been sweet and hot, her hands had been wicked, and he'd had his fingers deep inside her clenching heat mere steps from his own damned party.

"Right," she said. Drawled, really. And "disrespectful" didn't begin to cover the tone she used. Or that direct stare. "Because you would have opened a letter that I sent."

"Someone would have."

"And believed it right away, I'm sure."

"I don't believe it now, Miss Ransom. I'm not certain what you thought a personal visit would accomplish. All you have done is remind me of the low esteem in which I hold your entire family."

"I'm going to go out on a limb and guess that you don't have a lot of feelings about my poor grandma in Nebraska. I doubt you know about her at all, so lowly is her existence next to this whole…display." And Teo felt the umbrage of nearly twenty generations of de Luzes rise within him as she managed to do something with her face to indicate how little she thought of him, this grand house where history had been made and was still revered, and more or less everything he stood for. "So that low esteem, I'm guessing, is aimed directly at my mother."

"Your mother is little better than a terrorist," he retorted. Icily. "She sets herself a target, then destroys it."

"Yes," Amelia said drily. "This house is virtually rubble at our feet. It was the first thing I noticed."

"Once she got her claws in him, my father was never the same."

Teo discovered, with some consternation, that he was standing straight up from the desk when he hadn't meant to move. More, he was far too tense, with the temper she did not deserve to see kicking through him.

"My condolences." Amelia did not sound the least bit apologetic, much less sympathetic. "I must have misunderstood something. I thought he was Luis Calvo, the Eighteenth Duke of Marinceli, a man possessed of the same great wealth and immeasurable power you now wield. While my mother is...a mere divorcee. Who was the victim?"

"You must be joking. Calling Marie French 'a divorcee' is like calling a Tyrannosaurus rex a salamander."

Amelia's gaze flashed a deeper, darker shade of violet.

"There are very few things that I know to be incontrovertible truths," she said. And though her voice was soft enough, her gaze seemed to slap at him. "But one of them is that wealthy men fend off paternity suits the way a normal person slaps down mosquitoes on a summer night. Since our parents actually were married, no matter what opinions you have about that union, I thought I owed you the courtesy of telling you in person."

"Such courtesy. I am agog."

She turned all the way around to face him then, but if he thought she would lower her gaze meekly, it was his turn for disappointment. Amelia held his gaze steadily, and Teo could admit he found it...surprising.

Not discomfiting. He was the Duke. He was not *discomfited*.

But the truth was that most people did not dare hold his gaze. Or not for very long. Most people, as a matter of fact, treated Teo with the deference due his title.

A deference he had come to believe was due to him, personally, as the holder of the title, because of course it was no easy thing to quietly command an empire while pretending he did nothing but waft about to charity balls. Thrones were for the powerless in these supposedly egalitarian times, and the de Luzes had always trafficked in influence and strength.

Teo was somehow unsurprised that it would be this bedraggled American, daughter to a woman so coldly mercenary that she was her own cottage industry, who not only dared—but kept staring him down.

As if he was a challenge she could win.

But the fact he was not surprised did not mean he liked it.

"What is it you want, Amelia?" he asked, aware that his tone was cool. The word of a de Luz had once been law. These days it merely sounded like the law, which was close enough.

She blinked at him as if he was…obtuse.

It was not a sensation he often had.

"I've already told you what I want. What you need to hear, at any rate. That's all I wanted. To tell you."

"Out of the goodness of your heart. You wished to inform me of my supposed paternity, and then…what? Blow away like smoke in the wind?"

"Nothing quite so poetic. I thought I'd go back home to San Francisco. Try to enjoy the rest of my pregnancy and prepare for life as a single mother."

And she smiled sweetly at him, though he would have to truly be obtuse not to hear the decided lack of sweetness in her voice.

"I see. You are keeping this miraculous child, then?"

She tilted her head slightly to one side, her gaze quizzical. "I wouldn't trouble myself with coming all this way, then storming your very gate—literally—if I wasn't planning on keeping it. Would I?"

It was Teo's turn to smile. Like one of the swords that hung on his walls, relics of the wars his ancestors had won.

"It is with great pleasure, Miss Ransom, that I tell you I have not the slightest idea what you would or would not do in any given circumstance."

"Now you do."

"I'm taken aback, you see."

He had already straightened from his desk, and he suddenly found himself uncertain what to do with his hands. It was such a strange sensation that he frowned, then thrust his hands in the pockets of his trousers, as he would normally. It was almost as if he wanted to do something else with them.

But no. He might have shared a few explosive moments of pleasure with this woman—a circumstance he had yet to fully take on board—but he was a grown man stitched together with duties and responsibilities. He did not have the option to be led around by his urges.

"That must feel like a revolution," Amelia said. Rather tartly, to his ear. "What's next? Will the serfs rise up? Will they march on their feudal lord?"

"You seem to have mistaken the century."

"Right." Again, that insolent drawl. She made a great show of looking all around her, as if she could cast her glinting eye into every corner of the rambling house that had stood here—in one form or another—for so many centuries. "I'm the one stuck in the wrong century. Got it."

"What astounds me is the altruism of your claim," he said, finding his temper rather thinner than he liked. When normally he prided himself on being the sort of lion who did not concern himself overmuch with the existence of sheep, much less their opinions. "Out of the goodness of your heart, you chose to come here and share this news with me. That would make you the one woman in the world to claim she carries an heir to the Dukedom of Marinceli, yet has no apparent intention of claiming any piece of it."

"I'm hoping it's a girl, actually," the maddening woman responded. In a tone he would have called bland if he couldn't see her face. And that expression that seemed wired directly to the place where his temper beat at him, there beneath his skin. "If I remember my time here—and in truth, I prefer to block it out—there has never been a Duchess of Marinceli. Only Dukes. One after the next, toppling their way through history like loose cannons while pretending they're at the center of it."

His temper kicked harder. And he found he had to unclench his jaw to speak. "If you do not wish to make a bid for the dukedom, and you claim your only motivation is to inform me of this dubious claim of yours, I am again unclear why this required a personal audience."

"I was under the impression that this was the kind of thing that was best addressed in person," she said. Very distinctly. As if she thought he was slow. "Forgive me for daring to imagine that you might be an actual, real, live human being instead of this…caricature."

"I am the Duke of Marinceli. The doings of regular people do not concern me."

She rolled her eyes. At him.

Teo was so astonished at her temerity that he could only stare back at her.

"Noted," she said, in that bored, rude way that he remembered distinctly from her teen years. Though it seemed far more pointed now. "You are now informed. When you receive the legal documents, you can sign them happily and in private, and we can pretend this never happened."

"I beg your pardon? Legal documents?"

Amelia folded her arms, and regarded him steadily, as if he was challenging her in some way. And Teo was beginning to suspect that what beat in him was not strictly temper.

"Of course, legal documents," she chided him. *She* chided *him*. "What did you think? That I would trust you to let this go?"

"Let this go?" he repeated. And then he actually laughed. "Miss Ransom. Do you have any idea how many enterprising women, whether they have enjoyed access to my charms or not, take it upon themselves to claim that I have somehow fathered their child?"

"You're welcome to treat me like one of

them. In fact, I'd be perfectly happy if you thought I was lying."

Teo hadn't really made a determination, not yet. He hadn't let himself connect his mysterious redhead to this...disaster. Or he hadn't wanted to let himself. But there was something about the way she said that that kicked at him. As if she really, truly wanted him to dismiss her. And that was so different from the other women who had turned up over the course of his life to make their outlandish claims that it made something deep inside him...slide to the left. A simple, subtle shift.

But it changed everything.

"We will determine if you are lying the same way we determine any other claim," he managed to say despite that...shift.

"What does *that* mean? Ritual sacrifices? Forced marches? The dungeons?"

He lifted a brow. "A simple paternity test, Miss Ransom. The dungeons haven't been functional for at least a hundred years."

"I can take any test you like," she said after a moment. "Though that seems like a waste."

"Funnily enough, to me it doesn't seem like a waste at all. It seems critical."

She shrugged. "We can prove that you're the father if you like, but I'm only going to want you to sign documentation giving up your parental rights."

And something in him stuttered, then slammed down. Like the weight of the whole of this monstrous house he called his home, loved unreservedly and sometimes thought might well be the death of him.

"Miss Ransom," he said, making her name yet another icy weapon. "You cannot possibly believe that if you are indeed carrying my child—the firstborn child of the Nineteenth Duke of Marinceli—that I would abdicate my responsibilities. Perhaps your time here as a child—"

"Hardly a child. I was a teenager."

But Teo did not want to think about the teenager she'd been, too curvy and unconsciously ripe.

Had he noticed her then? He didn't think he had, but it was all muddled now. The girl he'd tried to ignore and the redheaded witch who had beguiled him into losing his head were tangled around each other and thrust, somehow, into this pale woman who stood before him with her blond hair flowing about her shoulders, not the faintest trace of makeup on her hauntingly pretty face, and eyes the color of bougainvillea.

He was forced to accept that it was not merely his temper that seethed in him.

But he kept speaking, as if she hadn't interrupted him. "Whatever age you were, we clearly failed to impress upon you the simple fact that the members of my family take their bloodlines very seriously indeed."

"I'm well aware." And there was something in her gaze then, and in the twist of her lips. It dawned on him, though he could hardly credit it, that the august lineage of his family was not, in fact, impressive to her. "But if I recall correctly, you're the person who, upon the occasion of our parents' wedding, loudly proclaimed your deep and abiding joy that my mother was too old to—how did you put it?—oh, yes. 'Pollute the blood with her spawn.' I can only assume that any child of mine would be similarly polluted at birth. You should disavow us both now, while you can still remain pristine."

It took Teo a long moment to identify the hot, distinctly uncomfortable sensation that rolled in him then. At twenty-six he'd had a sense of his own importance, but had imagined his own father would be immortal. His recollection of their parents' wedding—evidence that his once irreproachable father had lost it completely, a deep betrayal of everything Teo had ever been taught, and a slap against his mother's memory—was that he had been quietly disapproving. Not that he had actually said the things he'd thought out loud.

"I don't recall making such a toast," he said now. Stiffly. "Not because such sentiments are anathema to me, of course. But because it would be impolite."

"You didn't make a toast. Heaven forbid. But you did make sure I heard you say it to one of the other guests." And he might have thought that it hurt her feelings, but she disabused him of that notion in the next moment by aiming that edgy smile of hers at him. "In any case, I thought it would be *impolite* not to tell you about this pregnancy."

Teo didn't care for the way she emphasized that word.

"But it can end here," Amelia said, merrily. "No legal pollutants to the grand Marinceli line. I'm sure that in time, you'll find an appropriately inbred, blue-blooded heiress to pop out some overly titled and commensurately entitled heirs who will suit your high opinion of yourself much better."

Teo had never heard his duties to his title and his family's history broken down quite so disrespectfully before. It was…bracing, really. Like a blast of cleansing winter air after too long cooped up in an overheated room.

She claimed she was pregnant, and he couldn't dismiss the claim, because it seemed likely—however *impossible* and no matter how he wished it untrue—that she really had been the redheaded woman he had sampled the night of the Marinceli Masquerade.

More than sampled. He had been deep inside her, sunk to the hilt, and had woken the following morning wanting much, much more—another unusual sensation.

But this was not the time to lapse off into that cloud of lust—a cloud he now knew was deeply inappropriate and, if she was telling the truth about her pregnancy and his paternity, might well have already changed the course of his meticulously plotted life. It didn't matter why she'd come here or what game she was playing.

Teo wanted answers.

He prowled away from the desk, moving toward the chairs that sat before the fire. "Come in. Remove your coat. Sit, for a moment, as you deliver these little atom bombs of yours."

He made that sound like an invitation. A request. It was neither.

Amelia did not move. She stood where she was, still just inside the door, and...scowled at him.

Teo was certainly not used to people contorting their face into any but the most obsequious and servile expressions, but that, too, was not the issue here. He reached one of the chairs, and waved his hand at it.

"Sit, please," he said, and this time, it sounded far more like the order it was.

Amelia continued to scowl at him in obvious suspicion. But despite that, she moved closer. With obvious reluctance. In itself another insult.

"Most people consider it an honor to be in my presence," he told her drily.

She sniffed. "They must not know you."

And Teo's memory was returning to him, slowly but surely. He normally preferred to pretend those years hadn't happened. Those embarrassing, American years, when Marie French had draped herself over the priceless furniture, and laughed in that common, coarse way of hers. But now he had the faintest inklings of recollection where the daughter was concerned, and not only about those problematic curves.

Amelia had not faded quietly into the background, as would have been expected of any other girl her age. Not Marie French's daughter. He had the sudden, surprisingly uncomfortable memory of the uppity little chit mouthing off. Not only to him, which was unaccountable, but on occasion to his father, as well.

Which was unacceptable.

He couldn't say he much cared for either the recollection or a repeat of it now.

Amelia took her time moving across the floor, and then even more time shrugging out of her coat. Then, not to be outdone—and not to obey him totally under any circumstances—she then held it to her as if it was a shield as she sat down in the armchair Teo had indicated.

He took his time seating himself opposite her, putting together the pieces. If he squinted, he could see the pieces of the wild redhead who had made the tedious Masquerade that tradition insisted he throw far more entertaining than usual. He wished his body wasn't so delighted at her return. It could only cloud the issue all over again.

Amelia gripped that coat against the front of her, so hard he could see her hands become fists. "Do you need me to tell you how babies are made, Teo?"

"What possessed you to disguise your-self?" he asked coolly, choosing not to rise to her bait. Or choosing not to show her any reaction, anyway. "And not only disguise yourself, but as I recall, taking it upon your-self to make certain you got my attention. I would assume this was all part of an entrap-ment bid, but you claim you do not want my name, my money or any link to me whatso-ever. Explain yourself."

"I don't have to explain myself to you."

"And yet, Miss Ransom, you came to find me in my private home. One assumes to offer explanations, at the very least."

"I came to give you information. That's all. How many times do I have to say the same thing?"

Teo smiled, something raging in him, deep and dark. It wasn't as simple as temper. It was thick with that same lust, and wrapped around it, the possibility that the last person he had ever wished to see again might actu-ally have managed to trap him. *Him.*

A man raised to know better than to ever allow such a fate to befall him.

"Unfortunately for you," he told her, his voice a low lick of fury that rivaled the heat of the fire, "I don't believe a single thing you've said so far. Shall we start testing these claims of yours?"

"Test away," she said, daring to sound bored.

But he could see the heat in her gaze. She likely expected him to summon someone to administer a paternity test—and he'd get there.

First, he wanted to address that heat. And the redheaded woman he'd tried to dismiss from his mind—but hadn't.

"Wonderful," he said silkily. "Why don't we start with a reenactment of that night in September?"

"What?"

And he should likely not have felt triumphant that he'd finally managed to get a reaction from her.

But he did. And he was only getting started.

"Come over here, *cariña*," Teo said, and it was less an invitation than a command. "Straddle me the way you did then. Kiss me, this time without your mask. Let us see what truths there are to find without all these words, shall we?"

# CHAPTER THREE

HE DIDN'T THINK she would do it.

Amelia could see the certainty she would not in that dark gaze of his, threaded through with a hint of gold-plated skepticism. It was to be distinguished from his usual expression, which was far too haughty and aristocratic and *above it all* to actually be challenging— no matter how personally challenging she might have found it.

Teo clearly expected her to back off, or maybe he thought she would start flushing and stammering. Perhaps he expected her to start throwing things at him. Or to dissolve into a pool of tears.

She had the urge to do any number of those things, but didn't.

Because it hadn't escaped Amelia's notice that he still hadn't indicated that he believed her. Perhaps it wasn't a matter of belief, as far as he was concerned. It sounded as if she'd convinced him that she had been in disguise the night of the Masquerade. But she should have realized that a man of Teo's stature would never believe a pregnancy claim unless and until he saw it bolstered by cold, hard scientific evidence.

That meant that all of this—letting her into the house, allowing her into his presence—was all part and parcel of whatever game it was he'd thought he was playing when the butler had given him her name and announced her arrival. He could have had her tossed out with a snap of his fingers. He hadn't.

Whatever else was going on here, including her unfortunate reaction to him that she clearly hadn't exorcized at all, there was no doubt at all that *he* was playing a game. It allowed her to feel all the more ripe with the righteousness of *her* trip here, conducted beneath the mantle of her honesty.

If, that was, Amelia ignored the fact that she was the one who'd played games first. She was the one who had come here, taken what she'd wanted and disappeared. She'd left him none the wiser. The only reason he knew now was because she'd chosen to tell him.

She was the one who had chosen this. She was the one who controlled this.

*The last time you felt that way when Teo was involved, you ended up pregnant,* a voice inside her pointed out.

Amelia ignored that inconvenient fact, too.

She shoved her peacoat off her lap, then stood. Back in September, she'd worn a daringly cut gown that had been all about her cleavage and the glimpses each step offered of her thigh. Almost all of her thigh. She'd worn the highest heels she could walk in without killing herself, and because she wasn't *her*—because, for once, no one would look at her and make all the usual comparisons to her mother—she'd allowed herself to vamp it up.

Amelia had strutted around, welcoming the looks thrown her way when normally she would have gone to great lengths to make sure she blended, and as inoffensively as possible. She'd stood in provocative poses. She'd smiled recklessly and suggestively. She'd tried to channel her favorite screen sirens from way back as if she was trying out for one of those old movies she and her mother had loved to watch together, late at night in the many far-flung cities they'd flitted in and out of over the years.

It had been a delight, if she was honest.

She'd gotten Teo's attention, too. Then a whole lot more than his attention, and that had been...life-altering. Even before she'd learned that she was carrying his child. It had been a heavenly crucible, a stunning test of sensation and need, and she didn't regret a single second of it. She couldn't—not when she'd dreamed about what it would be like to touch him for so long.

But she also had his attention now.

Today she was resoundingly herself. She was wearing nothing but jeans, boots and the so-soft-it-was-basically-a-hug sweater her mother had given her for a birthday one year. She knew that rather than looking vampishly over the top, like an old movie, she looked as if she'd stayed up for far too many hours, packed into the middle seat of an overstuffed airplane.

But that look on Teo's face, for all its challenge and skepticism, was the same. As if he saw the same woman who had made him smile almost four months ago.

*The day you understand that sensuality is*

*strength, sweet girl, is the day you will finally be free,* Marie had always told her.

But Amelia had never understood it. Not until right now.

She shook her hair back from her face, and that, too, was different today. She'd spent hours creating her glossy waterfall of bright red curls for the Masquerade. This morning, all she'd bothered to do was take her hair down from the knot she'd tied it into for the flight. A glance in the rearview mirror of her hired car had suggested that it was a flat, lifeless disaster, and she'd felt unequal to the task of fixing it.

But still, Teo looked at her as if she was edible.

Amelia had the distinct impression that he didn't know it. And the man could make kings and topple governments with a phone call, but she was pretty sure that gave her the power here. Or at least *some* power, and with a man as effortlessly commanding as Teo, that was revolutionary.

She smoothed her hands over her sweater, molding it to her hips, in unconscious imitation of a sly little move she'd seen her mother make about forty thousand times. An unconscious move that became conscious the moment she did it, because she understood it now. Amelia had always liked to roll her eyes at her mother's various shenanigans around men, but it was different, here.

There was something about running her hands over her own curves while he watched. She could feel the heat spark and dance between them.

Amelia told herself that she could use it.

She picked her way across yet another thick, undoubtedly priceless rug. The only sound in the study was the crackle of the fire. The faint hint of winter outside when the windows rattled now and again.

And, of course, the deep kettle drum of her heartbeat—but she was hoping only she could hear that.

It could only have taken a moment to step across the space between their two chairs, but to Amelia, it seemed like one or two forevers, stitched together while the flames danced in the grate. And then she forgot about the fire, because she was standing before him, and Teo's black gaze was no longer simmering. It was a blast of fire.

"What was it you wanted me to do?" she asked, and she wasn't trying to sound sultry. Throaty.

But she did.

"I think you know." His voice was more silk than rough, and still, it seemed to have ridges as it smoothed its way over her.

And worse, she remembered.

First the dance. She'd affected a German accent, spicing up her Spanish. She'd dared him to ask her to dance, he'd acquiesced with that dangerous half smile, and it had really been all over then and there. The dance itself had been decorous enough. His hand had seemed so large splayed there at her lower back. And the way he'd held her fingers in his had made butterflies dance and swirl deep in her belly, as if they were performing their own daring waltz.

They had not spoken while they danced. It had almost seemed a shame, given the work she'd put into her carefully accented Spanish—

But there was too much heat. Dancing with him was like plugging herself in to some kind of generator. She felt the roar of it. The hum. And the longer they danced, the more she burned. Brighter and brighter, until she was certain she must have blinded the whole of the party.

Teo had never looked away.

When the music had stopped, he'd drawn her into one of the side hallways, down past yet another raft of astonishing paintings she recalled from a decade ago, then around the corner. That was where he'd pinned her to a wall and gotten his hands on her.

In her.

And she had come apart once already when he pulled her behind him into a room she wasn't sure she could find again if her life depended on it. That was how shaken she was. How deliriously, spectacularly torn apart.

It was there that he'd fallen back onto one of the sofas, then pulled her down onto his lap. And God help her, but for all her brave talk of exorcisms and getting on with her life, she still dreamed about it.

About the way his hands had cupped her cheeks, then pulled her mouth to his. About the glorious invasion, his tongue and hers, and never once the urge to balk. Never once that sense that she was kissing someone through a thick glass, incapable of feeling anything.

On the contrary, she'd felt too much.

It had all gone too fast. And taken forever, at the same time. He'd pushed her dress and her panties out of his way, handled his own trousers and the condom he'd produced from a pocket, and then had settled her on top of him.

And they'd stared at each other, caught in that electric intensity, as she'd taken the length of him inside her.

Inch by inch, slowly and carefully as if it was a seduction rather than a necessity for her, until they were flush against each other, his gaze was like the night, and she was stretched wide and deep to accommodate him.

She'd been too hot and too red, then, almost limp with the madness of it. That it was finally happening. That he was *inside* her. That she'd managed to handle him without him stopping, frowning and accusing her of being the virgin she was.

Amelia might even have taken a moment to congratulate herself for pulling it off.

But then he'd wrapped his hands around her hips, and taught her about rhythm. Pace. Depth and desire, and how very little she knew about…anything. Everything.

Teo had covered her mouth when she shattered. Then dipped his head to the crook of her neck when he followed.

She remembered all of that, in vivid detail.

So vivid she was sure she could feel it still. As if it had just happened. Moments ago, according to her body, which shivered into awareness. She felt the flesh between her legs ready itself for him, molten and soft.

Amelia had been so focused on her pregnancy. More accurately, on the stomach flu she couldn't seem to kick for all those weeks. Then the dawning realization she'd done her best to deny for as long as possible—coupled with a lot of desperate math.

And then, finally, the bitter truth she really hadn't wanted to face.

She had somehow forgotten…this. *Him*.

Teo.

And the reality of the effect he had on her.

If she was honest, it was the same effect he'd had on her when she was a teenager. The difference was, back then, she hadn't known what to call it. And more, he certainly hadn't shared her awareness of it the way he clearly did now.

"Do you need a refresher course?" he asked, and it was a taunt. The expression on his beautiful face was sheer arrogance, then. And yet in no way detracted from his appeal.

Nothing could.

This was where a wise woman would back

off. Say something pithy, perhaps. Cutting, certainly. What she certainly should not do was imagine that she could control this thing when she had already proven that she couldn't.

One of Teo's dark, smooth, outrageously haughty brows rose.

*He doesn't think you're going to do this,* she snapped at herself.

And it was bad enough that he was openly contemptuous of her mother. It was insulting that he considered himself so far above her that he could openly disparage her. Amelia thought she really might break into pieces, right here on his fancy ducal rug, if she backed down from this challenge.

She swung her leg wide, then slid herself onto his lap.

And it was a mistake. Obviously.

But it was so *hot.* He was so hard and muscled, lean everywhere, and he caught her around the back, hauling her close to him.

And it was just like September all over again. Their bodies came together like a key in a lock, and she was sure that she heard the dead bolt turn.

But whether it was opening or closing, she couldn't have said.

And she couldn't say she cared, either, because Teo was surrounding her then. He was so much bigger than her, and bigger than he should have been in his rich man's clothes that usually disguised far less impressive forms. His arms were dense with lean muscle and rock hard to the touch, and she had to fight to keep herself from shivering in a way she knew would be much too revealing.

Then again, did it matter? Because there was that gaze of his, dark and demanding, and she was certain that he could see her as clearly as if he'd turned her inside out. Again. Right here with the moody January day kicking around outside.

Amelia reminded herself that she might not be descended from almost twenty generations of near royalty like he was, but what she did have was a direct connection to one of the most desirable women who had ever lived. At least, if the roster of her ex-lovers was to be believed.

She made herself smile and hoped it was sultry instead of scared. "Remember me now?"

Teo took his time, as if he was searching her face for…something. Whatever it was, she didn't think he found it when that sensual mouth of his stayed grim.

"I do indeed." His dark gaze sharpened. "Perhaps you can explain to me why it is you felt the need to crash a party to which you were not invited, conceal your identity and go so far as to have sex with me when you must have known that had you introduced yourself by your actual name, I would have refused you."

Her throat felt dry, suddenly. And no matter how cool his voice was, or how unreadable his expression, she was tight against him. And he wasn't inside her, which meant that she could feel the truth, big and thick and hard between them. She would never know how she kept herself from shuddering.

In desperate, overwhelming need. And something far greedier.

"You are the Duke of Marinceli," she said, wishing she could make herself sound less… throaty. Less obvious. "Surely I can't be the first woman to go to great lengths for the mere taste of you."

He moved a hand, reaching out to run a thick hank of her hair through his fingers. He watched as he did it, so Amelia did, too. And that meant she was completely unprepared when he lifted his intense gaze to hers once more.

"You knew," he said softly. Dangerously. "You could be in no doubt as to my feelings about your mother."

"I know what you felt about my mother ten years ago," Amelia said, her heart kicking and her stomach cramping as if she'd tried to run a mile, or something equally foolish. "I had no idea what you felt about me. If anything."

"So you disguised yourself."

"I wanted to see if there was a connection. A spark."

He looked faintly horrified by the notion and she smiled, because these stuffy Europeans never seemed to understand that Americanness wasn't only unthinking gaucheness and naïveté as they imagined. It could be wielded as a weapon, like anything else.

"You know what it's like," she said, smiling wider. "Every little girl dreams of fairy tales. I realize you're a duke, not a prince, but who's to say there can't be such a thing as Duke Charming?"

She would have said that she'd never seen an expression of offended dignity before, though that probably wasn't completely accurate. But there was certainly no more perfect expression of it than Teo de Luz grappling with the fact that she had just called him... *Duke Charming*.

In all apparent sincerity.

"I had no idea you were so prissy about your title, Teo. And the deference you feel it ought to afford you." She shrugged, letting her smile go bland. "Are you really sure you want to claim a child who will be half Duke Charming the Nineteenth and the other half...me?"

"Miss Ransom." His voice was a sharp rebuke, and somehow, it didn't seem to matter that he was calling her *Miss Ransom* while she was straddling his arousal. While they were pressed together, having a ridiculous conversation, and pretending that nothing was happening between their bodies. No fire. No deep, raging need. "I would like to suggest, in the strongest possible terms, that you never call me such a thing again."

"What should I call you, then? My baby daddy?"

He actually winced. "Certainly not."

She shouldn't have laughed. "You really do make it too easy."

He shifted slightly then, and suddenly she felt that spiraling heat sharpen. And a delicious lassitude swept over her, reminding her of how she'd come apart in his hands.

Again and again.

"I hate to disappoint you," he growled. He actually *growled*. "Allow me to make it hard."

And then he slid a hand around the nape of her neck, angled his face over hers and took her mouth with his.

It was a punishment. It was a prayer.

And even though she was certain that she'd relived *exactly* this a thousand times or more, night after night, Amelia wasn't prepared. She had dimmed it, somehow. Imagined it differently. It was like pain, perhaps. She knew she'd experienced it, she remembered it, but she could never quite *feel* it again.

Because this made a mockery of fire.

This was a supernova.

He took her mouth with certainty. An impossible, consummate skill that made her head spin, and she liked it.

She more than *liked* it.

His other arm wrapped around her, his hand splayed wide as if he was trying to hold as much of her as he could. Her breasts were pressed against the wall of his chest, memory and reality clashing. Tangling. Circling around and around on top of each other until she could hardly distinguish one from the other.

Not that it mattered. Or she cared. He angled his head one way, then the other, tasting her and tempting her, making her surge against him to get more. Deeper. *Yes*.

And she was the one who had taken his bait. He had challenged her, and she'd let him. No one had made her come and sit here on his lap like this. She'd done it, imagining she had control, and now she was paying the price.

It was possible that the Duke of Marinceli wasn't the only arrogant person in the room.

His taste was exquisite. Male and addictive. And she was terribly afraid that those faint noises she could hear in the distance, somewhere, were coming from her own throat. Greedy, needy little sounds.

He kissed her and he kissed her, and then when she could do nothing at all but lose herself in the delirious slide of his tongue against hers, he moved. It took her a baffled, tumbling sort of moment to realize that he was standing up, carrying her with him. So that he supported her bottom on one hand, and her legs found their way to wrap around his waist.

He kept her there another moment, his mouth on hers in distinct possession.

And then he tore his mouth away from hers and set her on the ground before him.

She was afraid he knew exactly how wobbly her legs were beneath her. Her mouth felt swollen. She wasn't entirely sure that there weren't tears in her eyes.

"It is good to know where we stand, is it not?" His voice was silk and slap at once. "What astounds me about you, Miss Ransom, is that I do not think you are quite in control of yourself. Are you?"

"A kiss is just a kiss," she managed to say. "There's a whole song about it."

"Let me tell you what a kiss is today," he said, his voice controlled and even, and Amelia felt a daunting sense of horror as she realized that *he* was certainly not swept away. Or wobbling on his feet. On the contrary, his gaze was sharp and clear, as if he had only been toying with her all along. Her stomach knotted up. "A test, which you have failed."

"Are you sure that I'm the one who failed?" she asked, eyeing the front of his trousers with more bravado than boldness.

But Teo only looked savagely amused.

He moved away, over to his desk, where he swept up his mobile, scrolled for a moment, then typed something out. It took him another moment, then he tossed his mobile back down to the surface of his desk with a clatter.

"You're staring at me," he said, calmly. "And I know it is indelicate to say so, but you seem a bit…spun."

"I'm sure it's the jet lag."

"Here's what will happen." He was all ice and restraint and Amelia wanted to launch herself at him. Slap his face. Claw at his eyes. Behavior she would never condone in a million years, and yet… *Yet.* "I've texted my business manager. I told him another paternity test needs to be administered. I'm sure you will not be surprised to learn that there is protocol in place."

She felt thin and pale straight through, but she smiled. "How lovely to be so prepared for any eventuality."

"My manager will come with at least two members of my legal team, and they will see to the testing. I expect you to allow this test to be taken, but if you do not, never fear. That's why my legal team is involved. They will make certain that paternity is established, positively or negatively."

He didn't say *how* they would make certain, especially if she refused. But she didn't ask for clarification. She thought he wanted her to.

"If I'm not the father of the child you say you carry, or if, as often happens, you are somehow mistaken about your pregnancy in the first place, they will present you with a nondisclosure agreement to sign," Teo said. "Generally speaking, we encourage claimants to sign this agreement. We occasionally even sweeten the pot. My privacy is more important to me than money, which means I'm happy to spend it to make sure false claims against me are never discussed in public."

"Do you have protocol in place for when it turns out you *are* the father?" Amelia asked, impressed with the evenness of her tone when she felt like a giant, deafening scream inside. "Or do you just…wing it?"

His black eyes blazed. "I have every intention of following a very specific protocol if it turns out that you are, in fact, the mother of my child thanks to an act of egregious subterfuge. Believe me."

"I can't say I care what your protocol is, really. What matters is mine."

"You go right ahead and tell yourself that," Teo replied in that same dangerously silken tone. "I think you will find that the de Luz bloodline never, ever releases one of its own. Deny it all you wish. It will not change a thing. I have no intention of allowing any heir of mine to be raised apart from me."

"I don't want your influence. I don't want your money. I want nothing at all from you."

"Then, Miss Ransom—" and there was something in that gaze of his that made her quake, a kind of savagery that made her feel swollen with need "—you had better hope that this test comes back negative."

# CHAPTER FOUR

"YOUR EXCELLENCY." THE deferential voice came from the door.

Teo did not turn, though he inclined his head, knowing that his business manager would read the gesture for what it was: tacit permission to speak.

"The test is positive," the other man said.

For one beat of his heart, then the next, Teo was sure that he'd misheard. Because he must have misheard. "Positive?"

"Yes, sir. The child is yours."

Teo was still in his study, staring out at the winter version of the gardens that, come spring, the public clamored to fawn over on the few holidays he opened the grounds to visitors. But he hardly saw the landscape before him today. And not only because he knew it better than his own features.

His face changed with time, after all. The

grounds of the estate did not. Teo employed a battalion of gardeners and groundskeepers to make sure of it.

He cleared his throat.

"Thank you," he managed to say. "You may leave me now."

He waited until he heard the quiet sound of the door on the latch, and only then did he allow himself to breathe. Or whatever facsimile of breathing he was attempting to perform through the racket inside him.

Because he, Teo de Luz, who had watched his father wreak havoc with his reputation thanks to the terrible women he'd allowed near him—he, who had vowed that he would never, ever bring so much as the faintest stain to the august dukedom that was his to usher into the future, as bright and shining as possible—

*He* had fathered a child. Out of wedlock.

With Marie French's daughter.

Teo felt nearly light-headed with the potent combination of fury, despair and shame.

His life had always been plotted down to its smallest details. He had done the plotting himself. When he had come of age and understood both his place in the world and the importance of his bloodline, the debt he owed not only to his ancestors but to the long line of the descendants who must follow him, he had sat down and determined exactly what it was that he needed to do to accomplish those things. And how best to make certain that he did so with dignity.

He would become the Duke after his father. That was ensured.

But he had eighteen examples of the kind of Duke of Marinceli he could choose to become, with portraits to match that hung even now in his gallery. Teo had taken the various lessons of his ancestors' lives very seriously indeed.

It was all very well to have one child, the way his father had, and hope that the son he raised would be worthy of the gifts his birth accorded him. Teo had never been a gambler. He had no interest in risk. He planned to marry, produce an heir, and several spares besides. He did not wish to risk the possibility that the dukedom could fall to some far-flung cousin who had not been raised as he had been. Not if it was in his power to make it otherwise.

And not only because he liked the idea of continuing the bloodline through his direct descendants. For while he was avowedly arrogant, he was not quite *that* arrogant. What he truly wished was to make certain that he would have the opportunity to teach his own children what it meant to be members of the de Luz family. He would teach them what it meant to him, and in so doing, connect them with that long sweep of history and myth that was a part of who they were.

He wanted to fill them with as much gratitude as greatness.

He'd seen his future so clearly, always.

Even when his father had started his downward spiral into unsuitable women, it hadn't changed Teo's plans. How could it? He had never planned to look around for a wife until he was older, more settled and more capable of making certain that any wife he took would obey him as required. Because while Teo was fond of a spirited discussion when appropriate, there was only one true expert on the Marinceli legacy, and it was him. He'd accordingly spent a lot of time fashioning the perfect wife in his head, and she was not at all like the sensual redhead he'd indulged in last fall.

Certainly not.

His Duchess would be refined. Elegant in blood and action. Blameless, spotless and without a whisper of scandal attached to her name. Educated, dedicated and capable of assuming the duties that came with overseeing the Marinceli holdings and estates. He'd been thinking of a certain kind of heiress, bred for a life that looked like leisure—and certainly had its charms and compensations—but was often far more complicated than outsiders imagined.

He had always planned to marry a woman like his own mother.

His mother, who had given him softness where his father had given him duties. His mother, who had taught him the beauty of nature and how to find peace there no matter what. His mother, whom he had loved as fiercely as he loved the land and whom he had lost anyway.

And then lost again when his father had chosen to wash away her memory with a woman who was little better than a common streetwalker.

He had vowed he, by God, would honor his station and his mother's memory alike.

And now this. This…tragedy.

Because it didn't matter what Amelia Ransom said. Or what plans he might have made. The die was cast. She was carrying his child and that made her—*her*—the next Duchess of Marinceli.

Losing the appropriate heiress he'd planned to install here, to reclaim his mother's quiet glory in some small way, felt like losing her all over again.

Teo would marry Amelia, because it could go no other way. There was no alternative. The Dukes of Marinceli might divorce—or arrange timely accidents, in some centuries—but only after the line was secured.

And even then, rarely.

He glared out at his grounds, stretching on as far as the eye could see in every direction. But if he was looking for an escape, it was futile.

Teo had no choices here.

And in truth, he supposed it didn't matter. If he stepped back from his own reactions, there was something to be said for infusing an ancient family line with some literal new blood. Whatever else could be said about Americans, there was no denying that their brand of peasantry was…enterprising. The child would be hale and hardy and Teo would be on hand to guide him into his role as successor to the dukedom.

The question was, what was he to do with

this woman whom he was going to be forced to wed?

He turned, his gaze falling on the crackling fire. Something popped, and a log collapsed into ash and soot. And she'd spoken of fairy tales, had she not? Called him *Duke Charming*, perhaps the most nauseating thing he'd ever heard.

But as nauseated as the name made him, it did give him an idea.

Amelia liked fairy tales. He could give her one. After all, she was playing a deep game here that she'd started last fall, dressed as someone else—and in his experience, no one came after him who wasn't, ultimately, after his title. His wealth. His consequence, the very least.

She'd lived here when she was younger and he couldn't remember all the conversations that must have been had in her presence. About the dukedom, about Teo's role, about all the expectations and history heaped upon him. But he knew they must have taken place.

That made it hard to imagine that she didn't already know how this would go.

He would insist upon marrying her. He would insist on claiming his heir in the time-honored fashion, because outside the dukedom, it was the modern age—but here, always and forever, it was medieval. And the same rules applied now as had then.

Teo was sure Amelia knew all this. That he would do what was necessary to secure his bloodline, always.

But that didn't mean he had to make it pleasant for her.

If she wanted to play Cinderella games, he would be more than happy to oblige her.

Amelia had been taken off to one of the guest suites, carefully tucked away in the main part of the house, where a visitor could feel as if she was a part of things without ever straying into anything private.

First she had seen Teo's business manager, and a pair of lawyers, who had come in with perfunctory smiles and a sheaf of legal documents. Reading through those documents had taken more time than the actual physical she had also subjected herself to with the quietly competent doctor who'd accompanied them, and whom she recognized from her years here before.

*She* wasn't in any suspense. Amelia already knew who the father of her baby was.

Still, she'd had to sit there and look suitably grave as a pack of disapproving men had given her news that wasn't in any way news to *her*, but likely meant all kinds of things to *them*. Bless.

Then they'd all taken themselves off to handle the actual purpose of their visit—telling tales to Teo—though none of them said that directly.

"If you could wait here, madam," Teo's business manager murmured.

And when the door shut behind him, Amelia was faced with a decision.

The events of the morning were already a tumultuous jumble in her head. From the plane ride to that long drive to everything that had happened when she'd arrived here. She wanted to tell herself it all felt as if it had happened to someone else—

But she could still feel *him*. Vividly.

His taste was in her mouth again. She could feel that thick ridge of his need where their bodies had met. And she felt herself get soft and hot—even at the memory.

It made a mockery of her attempts to tell herself that she was immune to him. That she had somehow vaccinated herself against all things Teo de Luz.

And she was acutely aware, as she sat there

in the elegantly appointed living room of the suite where they'd left her, that nothing was holding her here. All those legal documents that she'd signed had been about protecting Teo in the event that she was not carrying his child. Very few had addressed the possibility that she might be, because, of course, no one had imagined that could be a possibility.

She'd known. And she'd told him. Now he had the additional proof he needed.

Amelia had absolutely no reason to sit here waiting for him to make good on the vague threats he'd already made.

But no matter how many times she thought the same thing, or told herself it was time to rise and go for the door, she didn't.

She waited.

She waited, and she waited, her eyelids getting heavier by the moment. And she couldn't have said when she fell asleep, exactly. One moment she was sitting there, fretting about when and how she should leave this place—and for good this time—and the next she was waking up in a rush, confused and faintly irritable.

The light in the room had changed, the shadows gone long and deep, and Teo stood over her. He stared down at her with a look on his face that she was tempted to call murderous.

Amelia told herself it was nothing more than the dreams she'd been having, one more intense than the last. She sat up, rubbing at her face, and looked around as if she expected to find someone else in the room with them. But no one else was there and she realized that whatever noise there was, it must all be in her head.

"What's happening?" she asked hearing the sleep in her voice.

The part of her that had been a notably awkward teenager in this same awe-inspiring house cringed at that, because if that was how she *sounded*, how must she *look*—but she had to shove that aside as best she could.

"We're having a baby," Teo said, and this time, that aristocratic voice of his was grim. It instantly put her on alert. "Allow me to extend my felicitations, Miss Ransom."

She was already frowning, so it was easy enough to sit up straight and slip on into a full-on scowl. "I think it might be time to stop calling me Miss Ransom, don't you? We didn't only have sex, Teo. We actually made another human life. I think the intimacy barrier has been well and truly broken."

He smiled, but it was a mirthless thing. "I took the liberty of having my security detail locate the vehicle you used to sneak onto my property."

"I didn't sneak. Just because no one regularly uses those old lanes doesn't mean driving on them is an act of subterfuge, does it?"

He ignored her. "I took the liberty of collecting your case."

She assumed he meant that he'd had a servant do it, as she couldn't imagine the Duke of Marinceli toting luggage about the place, and normally she would have pointed that out. Made a joke out of it—or a weapon. But the shadows in the room seemed darker than they should have been, her head was still full of jagged anxiety dreams, and she stayed quiet.

Teo studied her a moment, and it took all the self-control Amelia possessed to keep her hands from her face, to check for something embarrassing. "If you will follow me, we have a trip to take and it is already getting late."

He started for the door. Amelia stood automatically, then glanced out the windows. Sure enough, she'd slept most of the day away if the creeping dusk was any guide. And even though it was winter and sunset came early, it still seemed remarkably lazy on her part. She didn't normally succumb to jet leg, really. She'd discovered that no matter where she went on the planet, come three thirty in the afternoon of whatever time zone she found herself in, she was ravenously hungry. Other than that, she normally acclimated fine.

But everything was different in a pregnant body, she was discovering. She chose to be happy that the only symptom she was experiencing at the moment was some fatigue, here and there. It was better—anything was better—than the weeks upon weeks of nausea.

She was hurrying after Teo, out in the hallway and trying to catch up to his long strides, before she bothered to ask herself why. She didn't need to run around after him like a harried member of his vast staff. She didn't have to do anything with him at all, for that matter.

"Wait," she said, throwing the word at his back. "Why did you collect my bag?" Teo didn't stop walking. He didn't even look back over his shoulder. And it was as if, now that she was moving, Amelia couldn't quite bring herself to stop. "And what do you mean, we're going on a trip?"

"All will be revealed in good time," Teo

said, and there was something about the easy authority in his voice when he said it.

It was comforting, almost. As if he had the answers, when Amelia had spent the whole of her life in the presence of adults who never had answers, even when she was a child. She'd always been the one sent off to do her level best to find whatever answers were required. Even the great and powerful men her mother married turned to her when the relationship went bad, as it always did. Amelia always knew it was coming when the stepfathers or lovers suddenly showed a marked interest in taking her out to dinner, or to coffee, or invited her on a long walk out of the blue. These things always led to uncomfortable questions about her mother's favorite things. How best to talk to her. And as she got older, Amelia's own take on the situation—that situation being her mother's love life.

Having never experienced the opportunity to show anyone blind obedience, because she'd never trusted anyone with even wide-eyed, considered obedience, Amelia really hadn't understood how nice it was. Not to have to come up with the answers. Or a plan.

To trust that he had everything under control. Including her.

*You probably shouldn't find that liberating,* she chastised herself.

She followed Teo for miles and miles through the sprawling house. Then outside, briefly, to note the frigid slap of the January evening before climbing into a waiting car. Only then did it occur to her to ask herself—again—why this man made it seem perfectly reasonable to follow him off into the gathering night without the slightest idea where they were headed. Why she trusted him when she shouldn't.

But even as she asked herself the question, she knew the answer. The car pulled away, heading not toward the long drive that would lead them down to the gates and toward the village, but deeper into the property. And behind her, the magnificent house stood, lights blazing, *el monstruo* in all its glory.

And she understood that no matter how unimpressed she pretended to be with the Nineteenth Duke of Marinceli, the fact remained that he was safe, relatively speaking. He had kept this house wholly itself, and inarguably beautiful, when it could so easily have been turned into a tourist attraction. A hotel or event space. Or any of the other things aristocrats fallen on hard times liked to do with the old, stately homes that had once been the seat of their families' power.

She couldn't say she knew Teo well, only that she knew him in a variety of interesting ways. What she did know—what she'd known even as a teenager—was that he took his responsibilities very, very seriously.

If he was driving her off into the night alone, she might have worried. But she was carrying his child. And Amelia had to think that made her precious cargo to a man like him. Whatever he had planned, it couldn't be *too* bad.

Or anyway, it certainly wouldn't risk the child.

So she was very sedate, really, as the car pulled up to the private jet that waited for them on the estate's airfield. And it was the easiest thing in the world to climb aboard and settle herself inside, not at all surprised to find that Teo—unlike some of her mother's past lovers, tacky unto their very souls—preferred a quiet elegance even here. Nothing garish or over the top. Simply the height of comfort augmented by his tremendous wealth.

Because the more money a person had, the simpler the things they surrounded themselves with could be. If a person used it well, money was magic in reverse.

It was a short flight, but then, this was Europe. Everything could be reached quickly enough, and she had no idea how to even begin to figure out where they were as the plane landed. It seemed remote, if the few, scattered lights out her window were any indication on the way down.

Teo, who had disappeared into one of the staterooms for the flight, emerged. And she blinked, because unless she was hallucinating, the too-aristocratic-to-breathe Nineteenth Duke of Marinceli was…wearing jeans. And a T-shirt that she could only gape at before he tugged on the sort of wool sweater that looked better suited to northern fishermen than pampered Spanish dukes. He was even wearing winter boots, she realized in shock as she looked down at his feet.

But he was gazing at her, his dark eyes simmering and steady at once, and she refused to give him the satisfaction of asking.

Even if that meant she had to bite down hard on her own tongue.

Amelia expected the usual pomp and circumstance when they climbed down the stairs from the plane to the ground, but she found herself instead on a remote, abandoned strip of land that barely qualified as an airfield. It was dark, but she still had the sense of mountains looming all around. And it was *cold*. Bitter and harsh, not simply raw.

"Are we in the mountains?" she asked, as the cold cut into her. "Which mountains?"

"Welcome to the Pyrenees," Teo responded and he waited, there at the bottom of the jet's steps, as Amelia buttoned up her heavy peacoat and shuddered deeper into it.

And she didn't feel quite as comfortable or trusting or safe as she had before. But she followed him as he strode off into what seemed like nothing but darkness, her heart walloping her ribs from the inside, because what other choice did she have?

Luckily, all he was doing was walking over to an SUV that waited a little too far into the shadows for Amelia's peace of mind. There were no people. There wasn't even anything resembling an airport building. When she looked over her shoulder toward the plane, the jet was already pulling up its staircase, clearly readying itself to take off again.

With a sudden, prickling sense of foreboding, Amelia wanted to turn and run back for that plane. It was in her like a scream, the need to do it, to escape, to do anything but subject herself—

But she did nothing. And when Teo opened the passenger door of the SUV for her, with a mocking flourish, she even smiled.

She didn't smile again for some time.

Because Teo took to what passed for a road and all Amelia could do was grip the handle set in the door of the car and pray for deliverance.

The road wound around and around, barely wide enough for the car they were in at some points. The headlights picked up looming rock walls and catastrophic cliffs that tumbled down to God only knew where.

Teo didn't consult any directions. He simply drove, and she couldn't tell if he knew exactly where they were going, or if he was on some kind of a suicide mission. But no. She was revising her opinion on whether or not he was a murderer, but she still didn't think that he was likely to do away with... How had he put it? The heir to his dukedom. The Twentieth Duke of Marinceli, as a matter of fact.

Since the physician had let drop the fact that yes, it was a boy.

Amelia had vehemently not wanted to know—but now that she did know, it was as if she had always known that she was having a son. And she could hardly wait to meet him.

If she survived this car trip, that was.

Eventually, it ended. And not because Teo turned off somewhere or slowed down, but because the road simply…ended. And delivered them to what she thought was a gatekeeper's cottage, perhaps. It was a small sort of hut, hewn from wood and topped with layers of snow, and looked dark and unfriendly in the SUV's headlights.

Amelia expected one of Teo's staff to come out then and lead them somewhere else. But Teo turned off the engine, leaving the headlights bright. He sent a swift, shuttered look in her direction, then climbed out of the car.

And it turned out that she no longer felt any particular urge to follow him around. She stayed where she was, one hand creeping over that thickness in her belly that she knew, now, would be a little boy one day. She watched the father of that little boy—the *father*, which might be the correct thing to call him, but still felt a little too much, too intimate—march over to the front door of the little shack. He pulled something from his pocket that she understood was a key when he used it to open the front door. He disappeared, and for moment, there was nothing but darkness inside the hut, the headlights and Amelia's own too-fast breath.

Then, slowly she saw light inside. Moments later, Teo came back out. He switched off the headlights and pocketed the car keys, then went to the back of the SUV and she heard him removing things. And when he trudged past her, carrying not only her bag but several others, she finally stirred, and made herself get out of the SUV, too. Even if everything in her was telling her that was a mistake.

He'd left the front door open, so she pushed inside, not sure what she expected to see. And also not sure why the whole thing filled her with the greatest unease.

Inside, there was a fireplace that looked nothing short of medieval. It was large, a sort of grate stuck in the middle, and some kind of iron apparatus that held a pot over the flames. She was so struck by how archaic it was that it took her a moment to take in the rest.

It was a hut. A hunting cabin, maybe, if the decor was anything to go by. The fireplace was in what she supposed was the kitchen part of the great room. It boasted a small table, a counter next to the sink, and little else. The rest of the room was taken up with two very old leather couches, and a door behind them that led into the bedroom. She could see it was a bedroom because Teo was standing in there next to a large bed, doing something that didn't make sense. Until he straightened and she saw that he had lit a lantern.

A *lantern*. An actual *lantern*.

Her heart understood before she did, kicking wildly. She looked around again. The fire. A few lanterns here and there.

Unless she was mistaken, they were on top of a mountain with no electricity.

"Teo," she said when he came out of the bedroom, that enigmatic look on his beautiful face. "What are we doing here? Time traveling?"

And her pulse picked up when the Nineteenth Duke of Marinceli...smiled.

Like the spider to the fly.

# CHAPTER FIVE

*HE IS A DUKE, not a spider,* Amelia told herself crossly. *And you are certainly not a fly.*

But Teo's smile still made the back of her neck prickle.

"I come here at least once a year to escape the many pressures of modern life," he told her, his voice cool and unbothered in a way that she found very nearly offensive. Especially as he prowled back into the great room and settled himself on the couch facing the door. In a decidedly leisurely fashion. "I hunt for my food or make my own meals from what's on hand, I marinate in the silence of nature, and I often learn a great many things about myself. I can't recommend it highly enough."

Amelia lived in California. She could talk about *communing with nature* around the clock without batting an eye…but not with Teo.

"You thought that it was time for us to go on a rustic retreat?" she asked, her voice much too high-pitched. Because she wasn't really taking this the way she was sure she was supposed to. Then again, how was someone supposed to take this?

"I don't know how you will enjoy the accommodations," Teo continued. He looked almost smug, she thought. Entirely too self-satisfied, and something cold trickled down the length of her spine. "*If* you will enjoy the remoteness. But I can't say I particularly care. You are carrying the heir to the Marinceli dukedom."

"Yes, Teo. I was already aware of this when we were still standing in your other antique property. You know. The one with electricity."

"The trouble with all my other properties is that they're too connected to modernity," he said, almost as if he was musing his way through this conversation. When the look in his dark eyes suggested otherwise. "Up here, there is nothing between a person and her God. Ample time and space to reflect."

"I have nothing to reflect on, but thank you."

And she could hear that higher pitch in her

voice with her own ears. Again. She refused to call it hysteria, but it sure was close.

Teo moved farther into the room, and tossed himself down on one of the couches. "We will do our reflecting together, I think."

"What?"

He smiled at her, but again, it wasn't any kind of nice smile. It reminded her that he was directly related to warlords. To men who stood in the shadows behind kings, dark puppet masters who never minded that the light shone elsewhere.

"All my life I have done my best to avoid this moment, Miss—" But he stopped. That smile of his deepened, and that definitely wasn't good. "Excuse me, *Amelia*. And yet here I am. Well and truly trapped into something you knew perfectly well I would never have wanted if I'd had any choice."

"We both saw you use a condom," she gritted out. "If you're trying to say I tricked you by deliberately getting pregnant, you'll have to explain to me how I managed to do that when you're the one who had the condom, put it on and supposedly knew how to use it."

She was perilously close to telling him that she'd been a virgin that night—and Amelia didn't want to go *there*. It felt like a weapon, but one that could be used against her. She swallowed it down.

Teo was watching her in that same cold, considering way that she was beginning to understand was where he hid his temper. "We would not be having this discussion if I had known who you were last September."

"That doesn't—"

"Stop, please."

He didn't raise his voice. He didn't need to. Her tongue seemed to stop of its own accord, freezing there in her own mouth.

And it occurred to Amelia that she'd thought she'd seen all the power this man carried with such offhanded grace. That she'd made a study of it. Of him.

When the truth was, she'd had absolutely no idea.

Until now.

Here, in a bare-bones shack stuck on the top of a mountain in the middle of Europe. Without the slightest possibility that she could get help. There wasn't only no electricity, there appeared to be no phone lines. A quick glance told her there was no cell phone signal.

There was nothing but him.

It turned out that panic tasted metallic.

"I am not going to argue with you about

what happened," Teo said in that same soft yet thunderous voice. "I do not wish to hear evasions or excuses, and it wouldn't matter what you said in any case. We both know what you did."

She found her hands on her belly again, and his gaze dropped to track the movement.

It felt shocking. Like a touch.

"And now here you are, Amelia." He sounded as dark as the cold night that had fallen hard outside, and her name in his mouth made something deep inside her quiver. "Pregnant with my child."

Amelia took a breath, aware that she was standing inside the door of a place this man owned, again. Just as she had earlier, she felt very much as if she'd been summoned to see the headmaster. It was probably a good moment to remind herself that she hadn't been. There was no headmaster here.

Teo might be the Duke of Everything and Then Some, but he wasn't the boss of her.

She looked back over her shoulder, through the door that still stood open. But she knew he hadn't left the keys in the SUV, so she didn't bother to race for it. She slammed the heavy front door shut, which had an instant result, both positive and negative.

In the positive column, it was significantly warmer. Instantly and happily.

But the downside of that was that she was now standing sealed in a room with Teo.

She shrugged out of her coat and tossed it on one of the kitchen chairs, then took her sweet time sauntering over to sit on the couch opposite him, stretching out her feet just as he was doing.

As if neither one of them had a single care in the world.

"Forgive me, Your Excellency," she murmured, smiling edgily right back at him. "But this is starting to feel an awful lot like a kidnapping."

Teo did something with a single finger that might as well have been a shrug. "You can call it what you like. I brought you here because it is such an excellent place for…contemplation."

He wanted her to react to the emphasis he put on that last word, obviously. So, clearly, she refused to give him the satisfaction.

Amelia gazed back at him steadily. "I live in San Francisco. I enjoy contemplation as much as the next girl. But somehow, I'm getting the feeling that this is rather more of a guided meditation than an opportunity to pursue my own thoughts."

"This is the situation before us, *cariña*," he said, and the endearment was like a scrape. Because he wasn't above infusing it with all that sharp, acid mockery. Amelia hated that it got to her. "The Marinceli heir cannot be born out of wedlock."

"I'm not marrying you."

"This has nothing to do with preference or inclination. It is a simple statement of fact. My child—my son—will be the next Duke. The Twentieth Duke. Not only must he be born with my name, he must be raised to uphold the traditions that come with it. And he must learn a great, bone-deep awe for the responsibilities inherent in his position."

"I'm not marrying you, and you're certainly not raising my baby."

She only realized she sounded a shade too shrill when Teo's eyes gleamed with what she was terribly afraid was satisfaction. Especially when he relaxed back against the leather.

"It will perhaps not surprise you to learn that you are not the first reluctant Marinceli bride," he said after a moment, his voice... more caressing, somehow. "Some say a reluctant bride is what spurred the first Duke to build what would later become the family home… *El monstruo* was as fine a prison as he could make her."

Amelia lectured herself against the odd sensation in her jaw—and throughout her body—that made her teeth want to chatter. And then shake her, everywhere.

"You're not listening to me, Teo," she made herself say, in repressive tones. "There will be no wedding. I made a vow a long time ago that I would never get married."

"I vowed I would never touch Marie French or anyone associated with her." He really did shrug, then. "Vows are made to be broken, apparently."

"I should probably tell you now, but I have a very strict rule about dating only normal men," Amelia continued as if she hadn't heard him. "Regular, down-to-earth men who think a typical first date is meeting for coffee. In an actual coffeehouse, where you have to pay entirely too much money to drink burnt coffee and eat insipid pastries. That's a *good* first date, Teo. It doesn't involve security details. Or stately homes. Or more titles than sense."

"Or, to pick an example at random, disguising oneself and seducing the unwary."

She laughed. "I would never call a man with your investment portfolio *unwary*."

"Is that the appeal of the date you described? Because I prefer dating women who require more from me than an insipid croissant."

That frozen, almost affronted look on his face suggested she was lacking, somehow, in not being one of those women.

"The thing about being around very wealthy people for a lifetime is that it ruins the mystique of it all." Amelia lifted a shoulder, then dropped it, in a delicate sort of shrug that she'd seen her mother perform a thousand times. "I want credit card debt, pizza takeaways and a real, decent man who wants me for me. No trophies, no talk of bloodlines, just…a normal life."

His lip didn't *actually* curl. "That sounds like a remarkably squalid fantasy."

"You don't have to fantasize about it, then."

"Whereas you can fantasize about it all you wish," Teo replied silkily. "But it won't change a thing. You will marry me. You will become the Duchess of Marinceli, and if you think it gives me any pleasure to say this, you are gravely mistaken."

She would not pay attention to the teenager

inside her, who shriveled into the fetal position at that. The teenager who had wanted nothing so much as Teo's approval and affection, no matter how unlikely it was she might ever witness either. Much less receive it.

Not being that teenager any longer came with a great many benefits. And one of them was not letting that hurt her.

Much.

"It must be some kind of pleasure," she said, pleased when she sounded as unbothered as he did, "or you would not have abducted me, marooned me on the top of a mountain, and then think it made perfect sense to sit around making pronouncements."

"You have a mouth on you." And something flickered in Teo's dark eyes that made her catch her breath. And wonder if she would ever let it go again. "You had it when you were a child. I see time and maturity have done absolutely nothing to temper it."

She sniffed. "All the more reason you shouldn't marry this untempered mess, then."

And she almost believed what she was saying. She could almost convince herself that she was as blasé about this whole situation as she should have been. *Almost.*

"You are beneath me in every possible

way," Teo said, so lightly that it took her a moment to register what he'd said. And that bright fury in his gaze. "It is a humiliation almost beyond bearing that I should be forced to sully my name, my station and the whole of the Marinceli bloodline with the daughter of a known mercenary."

That, too, he said so politely, so quietly, that it was tempting to imagine she'd misheard him.

"Not just any mercenary, out to dig for whatever gold she might find, but *Marie French*," he said, and there was nothing soft about the way he said her mother's name then. His eyes flashed. "But there is nothing to be done. You chose to do what you did, it is done, and now we both must pay the price for the rest of our lives."

His conversational tone made insult into injury. As if this was hardly worth discussing. As if it was simple fact.

As if she was a bit dim and very foolish indeed not to have acquiesced already.

"You're not such a prize yourself," she retorted.

But all Teo did was laugh.

"I am far more than a mere *prize*, Amelia. And well you know it." He laughed again, though there was more offended astonishment than amusement in the sound. "The price you have to pay for the actions you took is an almost inconceivable elevation in status you in no way deserve. An unfathomable reward. I can't think of a single member of any royal family in Europe who would not consider it a privilege to become a Marinceli, and instead *el monstruo* may well crumble to dust in protest after all."

Amelia was shaking again, but this time she knew full well it was temper, not temptation.

"I'm not sure I'm getting your point," Amelia said, not bothering to conceal the edge in her voice. "It *almost* seems as if you're suggesting that I'm beneath you in some way? I can't really tell. Maybe you could give me more insulting examples."

"It is what it is," Teo said, with another aristocratic shrug. "The bloodline will no doubt be improved by the application of all this unexpected…"

"Peasantry?"

His eyes gleamed again, and Amelia really, really wished she couldn't *feel* that the way she did. Inside and out.

"None of this matters," Teo said, back to

silken menace. "We have months yet before you will bring my heir into the world. Ample time, in my opinion, to concentrate on what is truly at stake."

"My child is the only thing at stake, obviously," she threw back at him. "Or I would be safe at home in my apartment in San Francisco, happily continuing to forget you exist."

He watched her as if she was an exhibit in a rather distressing zoo. "Can you categorically state that you did not deliberately go out of your way to create this situation?"

"I didn't set out to have your baby, if that's what you mean." She'd set out to do something else entirely, but she couldn't quite bring herself to say that. Not here, when they were the only people around for miles, and he had that knowing look about him that made her think he already knew everything already. "This pregnancy was a complete shock. Whether you believe it or not, it was an accident. But let's you and I be really clear about something, Teo. The child—*my* child—will not be."

But Teo was sitting forward, that black-gold gaze tight on her. "You didn't deliberately entrap me into this in a bid to enrich yourself. Is that what you're saying?"

"Yes, you've found me out. What I wanted most in this world was to link myself to a man who hates me but will force me to marry him anyway. A man who cares more about his bloodline than is at all healthy and proves that by a spot of kidnapping to liven up a January evening."

"It is a pity, Amelia, that I am not convinced."

"I would rather die than spend the rest of the night with you, much less the rest of my life," she hurled at him.

With, she could admit, a lot more of that poor, brokenhearted teenager inside her than she wanted to admit.

But His Excellency didn't erupt into arrogance.

"No need to fling yourself off the side of the mountain," he said drily instead. "Especially not as now, I'll be forced to save you." He waved a languid ducal hand, taking in the whole of the cabin around them. The jagged peaks outside. The snow and the dark. "Consider this your chance to prove yourself to me. There is nothing for miles in any direction but you and me. No hint of wealth or consequence to be found. I would expect a typical gold digger, like—"

"If you say like my mother, I won't be held responsible for my actions."

Teo nodded, though it wasn't any kind of surrender. More like noblesse oblige.

"You may have forced us into this," he said instead. "But that doesn't mean you get what you want."

"Clearly."

"We'll stay here as long as it takes," he said quietly. "If you didn't plan this to extort me, it's your opportunity to show it."

She shook her head. "And if I feel no particular need to prove myself to anyone, thank you, because I'm a grown woman who doesn't actually require your approval to take her next breath?"

Teo considered her, all black-gold flame and that stern mouth of his. "Then, *cariña*, I fear you are in for a very hard winter."

# CHAPTER SIX

AT FIRST SHE clearly thought he was kidding.

"We're not staying here all winter," she said.

"Are we not? That is entirely up to you, Amelia."

And Teo watched impassively as she stared back at him, obviously waiting for the other shoe to drop. For the punch line to roll out and break the tension.

Instead, he gazed back at her and let the moment stretch out.

He had no intention of making things easier on her.

Especially because the more he looked at her, the less he understood how he had failed to recognize her last fall. She'd worn very bright lipstick, it was true, but there was no disguising that lush, sensual mouth.

There never had been.

And it settled on him, with a weight he

wouldn't call *heavy*, exactly, that this was the first time he could indulge himself when he looked at her. She was no longer too young. She wasn't his stepsister. And she wasn't wearing a theatrical mask to hide behind.

Teo had already resigned himself to the fact that she was carrying his son. He knew all the implications. He had always known precisely who and what he was.

And the longer she stared back at him, trying to read his intentions, the more he became aware of something else in him that he suspected had been there a good, long while. A heat that seemed to grow into a kind of roar

But he was not a man who succumbed to his passions. The only time he could remember doing so, in fact, was last fall at the Masquerade.

The Duke of Marinceli was expected to play host at the Masquerade, not nip off into a private room with a strange woman. Teo had never allowed himself such spontaneity. His entire life was a monument to plotting, planning and premeditation.

He had not said anything in that quiet drawing room when the passion between them had been spent. He had hardly known himself. He'd watched his masked redhead as she smiled at him. Had he recognized that mouth of hers even then? Was that the reason her smile had settled so heavily on him, like a reprimand?

She had slipped from the room. And Teo had not been sorry to discover that when he rejoined the ball, she had disappeared. He'd been less sanguine when he'd woken the following morning as hungry for her as if none of that had happened.

Teo had spent the months since assuring himself that one small indiscretion could not possibly count against the backdrop of a lifetime of responsibility. He had been *certain*.

And now he was here. With her.

Worse, it was more difficult by the moment to convince himself that his body wasn't having the same enthusiastic response to her that had gotten him into this mess in the first place. Something he would have been happy to blame on a spectacular woman dressed to cause a riot, the way she had been at the Masquerade.

But Amelia wasn't dressed to do much of anything today, unless it was to highlight her general unsuitability for the role her pregnancy had thrust upon the both of them. Teo had not imagined his wife—his Duchess—in the sort of clothing a regular person could obtain at one of the strange shopping malls they apparently favored. He had certainly never entertained the notion that she might be an American.

And if he allowed himself to think about Marie French again, he didn't know what he might do—

He stopped.

He let the silence between them drag on, and thought about the situation he'd created for the two of them instead.

This cabin had been a favorite retreat of his grandfather, the Seventeenth Duke. He'd kept it stocked with essentials, including the whiskey he preferred in the evenings—and that Teo only permitted himself to sample here.

He stood, enjoying the way Amelia stiffened as if she was bracing herself for an attack, and went to help himself. Then he selected a book from the broad, sprawling collection generations of his ancestors had left here for nights like this, and then settled himself in by the fire to enjoy a peaceful evening.

Or to appear to enjoy a peaceful evening, as if he didn't care what she did—when the truth was he was aware of every breath she took.

Entirely too aware.

"You're…just going to sit there and read?" she asked at one point, sounding strangled.

He'd taken his time looking at her. "What else do you suggest I do?"

And he'd enjoyed the way she flushed far too much.

When he was ready to take himself to bed, he did so without further comment, leaving her to her own devices. He heard her start to say something, then bite it back.

Uncertainty could only make the seriousness of their situation more clear to her, he told himself, feeling very nearly self-congratulatory as he climbed into the bed. And if this gambit of his had more to do with revenge? He was fine with that, too.

He kept telling himself that as he lay there in bed, glaring at the ceiling, everything inside him tense and too hot. He decided it was fury, because it should have been.

Because she was going to marry him, sooner or later, and he didn't know if he was more insulted at the prospect of marrying so below himself—or at the fact *she* seemed more insulted than he was.

Because his life had taken a drastic left turn when it was meant to proceed as a gentle, straight line—when he'd gone to great lengths to make sure it did—and it was all her fault. It was that damned dress she'd worn. It was her bright red lips and the molten heat of her.

He played and replayed that night last fall in his head, which was not helpful. And he tried to make himself forget that she was just there, in the next room...

Also not helpful. Or successful.

And Teo was not at all surprised, come the dawn when he finally gave up on his restless sleep, to find her curled up in a ball on the sofa where he'd left her. There were empty wrappers of nutrition bars on the table, telling him what she'd had as her dinner. She'd piled a selection of throws on top of her to keep her warm, which tugged at him in ways he planned to ignore, and had let the fire go out.

It struck him as an excellent opportunity to educate her in how this little retreat of theirs was going to go.

And maybe he took a little too much pleasure in waking her up, keeping his voice and expression stern as he asked her what she thought she was doing.

"It's winter in the mountains," Teo continued, staring down at her as she blinked sleepily, then looked around in confusion. "You cannot allow the fire to go out, Amelia. Surely a woman who plans to give birth to a child—and presumably care for it and keep it alive and well—should have better survival skills."

She was still wearing her clothes from the day before. Her long blond hair was in a glorious snarl, and she only shoved it out of her way as she pushed herself up to sitting position. Then she frowned at him. Blearily.

And there wasn't a single part of that he should have found attractive. Or appealing. She was common. Unrefined. A pageant of inelegant, indecorous vulgarity.

But tell that to the hardest part of him.

"I wasn't planning on raising my child in a shack on the top of the mountain, actually," she said, adding that knee-jerk defiance of hers to the list of her sins. That she was not impressed with him or his position and consequence was clear.

He found her...confounding.

"Is it that you don't know how to build a fire?" he asked, folding his arms and making his voice into granite. "I find this difficult to believe. Surely you must have *some* use."

"I have never built a fire, no," she said, "because I prefer to gaze at nature from afar rather than fling myself into the midst of it and hope for the best."

He only stared at her, fascinated against his will by that stubborn jaw of hers. And the echo of that mulishness in her sleepy gaze, a thick purple at this hour.

"I don't camp," she said. "My skills run more to finance and asset allocation, not to mention good old-fashioned companionship. Fire starting never seems to be on the menu."

"Of course not. Because why would Marie French teach her daughter anything useful?"

"Your obsession with my mother is not a good look," Amelia said mildly. It was only that brighter gleam in her eyes that told him the truth about her temper. "Though it's humanizing, certainly. In the sense that it makes you just as boring and run-of-the-mill as any other man I've ever met."

She was trying to get under his skin, and what irritated Teo was that it was successful. More successful than he wanted to admit, in fact. But that didn't mean he had to show *her* that it was working.

The trouble with Marie French wasn't only that she'd married his father, both usurping and staining his mother's memory. Because there were a number of women who had done the same thing after she had whom he disliked, but not with this same fervor. And it wasn't only that Marie's station was so decidedly below the de Luzes, though that had certainly always confounded him. His problem was that his father had been besotted with her in a way that the old Duke had never been with anyone else. Including Teo's mother.

That wasn't something he intended to forgive.

No matter that he was now bound to the daughter, with chains he knew he'd never break.

Even if they choked him.

"Let me explain to you how this will work," he said, looking down at her, and he was sure that he could see her fight to stay where she was. That jaw of hers tensed farther, and he flattered himself that she was struggling with her urge to leap to her feet and face him on more equal footing. "You have two choices."

"Choices? What choices? I thought you relieved me of such things when you abducted me yesterday."

He didn't smile, exactly. "There are always choices, *cariña*. They may not be good choices, but they always exist."

"This is pointless." Amelia rubbed at her face. Then scowled at him, as if she'd been hoping that he was a bad dream and if she rubbed her eyes, he'd go away. "You must know that I don't want to marry you. I certainly don't want to coparent with you."

"I beg your pardon? *Coparent?*" He pronounced the word as if it offended him. It did. "I am unaware of any such designation, thank you. I plan to parent my child, personally and completely. It does not require a prefix."

"Funny, I remember your father talking about the fleet of nannies who raised *you*," she replied. "And if memory serves, you felt you had been raised beautifully. So did he."

"I am not my father."

And it was not until his words hung there between them that Teo understood how profoundly he meant that.

But that wasn't something he planned to excavate at dawn. With the daughter of the woman who had singlehandedly ruined the old man.

"You can lock me away for the rest of my life and I won't change my mind," Amelia was saying, her voice ringing as if she was making her own vows.

Teo only smiled. Darkly. "Then I fear we will stay here a very long time indeed."

She regarded him steadily, though certainly

not politely. "I thought you were offering me choices. Not a prison sentence."

"A prison is a prison, Amelia, and you chose these bars when you decided to sneak into my party and deceive me last fall." He dared her to look away, but she didn't. And that only made him want to reach out and get his hands on her again—the very opposite of what he should have wanted. "It is up to you how you would like to serve your time, that is all."

"How appealing." Her voice was crisp, her violet gaze sharp. "It's becoming less and less of a mystery how the most eligible bachelor in the world has remained single and unattached all this time."

Teo did not spend a great deal of time questioning himself. There was no need—he was the Duke. That was the beginning and the end of it and there was no one in his life who dared question him.

Much less mock him.

To his face.

He could not say he enjoyed the experience, not least because it forced him to face the fact that he was perhaps more precious than he'd always imagined he was. Because for a hot, wild moment, all he could focus on was his need to make her pay for her temerity—and surely a man of his stature should have been secure enough in his place to laugh off rudeness and slights alike.

Then again, the method of payment he had in mind had nothing to do with laughter.

He reminded himself that he had not brought her here, to the very top of a mountain his family had owned since the Crown of Aragon ruled the area in the twelfth century, to concern himself with her rudeness. It was her defiance he intended to conquer.

And would. Because his firstborn son would have his name. There was no other option.

"We have a certain chemistry," he said now, which struck him as a vast understatement. The mouth he had so enjoyed last fall, so luscious and red, should not have called to him as it did now. Bare and unsmiling. Her hair a disaster. Her gaze insolent at best. "Some marriages start with far less than that."

"Marriages that took place in the first century, perhaps." Amelia pushed to her feet then, bringing the soft throw with her and clutching it to her chest as if she was preserving her modesty. When she was still wearing all her clothes. "I understand that the Marinceli family is stuck in the past. But that doesn't mean you have to stay there, Teo. Or that you have to drag me down with you."

He'd been standing there over the sofa, looking down at her. And a gentleman would have stepped back as she rose, to give her space.

Teo had been raised a gentleman, but that didn't seem to apply here. He couldn't seem to access the manners that had been imprinted on him so long ago they were usually second nature to him. He didn't move—and was instantly rewarded for that with the simple pleasure of watching her tilt her chin up. Then tip her head even farther back so she could raise her gaze to his—all the way up to where he towered above her.

He liked the way her cheeks flushed. And the way that curiously magnetic temper of hers lit the violet of her eyes, making them gleam all the brighter.

"The Marinceli family is timeless," Teo said, almost amused. "It doesn't matter what century it is, we endure."

"Is that one of my choices? Because I'll go ahead and pass on *enduring* right now. That sounds like a joyless march to a grim death. No, thank you."

Teo blinked. *No, thank you* was not the typical response to any offer he made. It certainly wasn't the expected reaction to an invitation to join the family. This woman was maddening.

He wanted to believe she was simply ignorant, but she had spent those years in Spain. With his father, and with him, too. There was no question that she might not know precisely who and what the Marincelis were.

Teo was perilously close to losing his self-control. "When you are ready to stop this foolishness, accept reality and take your place at my side, you are welcome to sleep with me in the bed."

He watched the pulse in the base of her neck go wild. He felt an answering beat in his own neck. And far lower, where he was too hard, too ready.

Amelia took her time swallowing, delicate and deliberate at once. "You're saying you want me to have sex with you."

"Oh, yes," he said, his voice low. Dark and rich. "A great deal of sex, one can only hope. Have we not already demonstrated that that is what we do best?"

"We've demonstrated that we *can* do it," she shot back. "But whether or not the one time makes it *the best*, I couldn't possibly say."

"I can think of a way to find out."

Amelia sniffed as if the notion revolted her, but he was still too close to her. He could see the truth in her flushed skin, her dilated eyes.

"I get to sleep in the bed only if we're having sex. Am I getting the terms of your little blackmail attempt right?"

Teo shrugged as if he didn't care either way. He felt that he really shouldn't have cared either way, but that did not appear to be in the cards.

"It's not a blackmail attempt, *cariña*. It's a choice. If you wish to share the bed, you must consider it the marital bed. That hardly seems unfair."

"I have no intention of marrying you," she said, with insulting directness. "Or sharing a bed with you. Under any circumstances whatsoever, Teo."

"That is a pity," he said coolly. "If you share the marital bed, I will treat you as my Duchess. And we will enjoy a rustic retreat together ahead of our wedding. If you do not—"

"I won't. Ever."

"If you say so."

"I would stake my life on it," she threw at him.

He nodded. Sagely. "Then you may sleep on this couch, and I will treat you like a servant."

"Is this a good time to talk about what's wrong with you? And how women can actually be more than your Duchess or your maid?"

"*Women* can be anything they like," Teo retorted, his tone harsh. "You have fewer choices because you stole mine."

It was a grim victory, certainly, but a victory nonetheless when she paled. And didn't throw something back at him, for once.

He chose not to point out that she'd already differentiated herself from her mother. Since Maric French was shameless, through and through, as Teo had personally witnessed in the dark days of her marriage to his father.

"I expect the fire to remain lit, if banked, at all times, as I do not wish to freeze to death. I expect three meals a day, and you may rejoice in my benevolence, as I expect very little in the way of haute cuisine here."

"Oh, happy day," she muttered. No longer quite so pale.

"And this might be the most difficult for you, Amelia," he continued. "But I expect deference."

"I expect you to go to hell," she shot back.

"I'm afraid I insist on courtesy," he said, almost sadly. "And if I were you, I'd figure out how to obey. Before I lose my good humor altogether."

# CHAPTER SEVEN

"I THINK YOU'VE forgotten that there's also a third option," Amelia managed to say, somehow *not* commenting on Teo's supposed "good humor." Though it was hard to get the words out through gritted teeth. And a jaw so tight she was worried it might shatter at any moment. "I could also do neither of those things. I could sit back down on this couch, ignore you and wait for you to tire of whatever game this is."

"You could," he agreed, but there was something far too dangerous in the way he said it. It shivered through her, far more intense than a mere dare. "But I'm a simple man, particularly here. If you are not functioning as a servant, I will only be able to recognize you as the woman who is to be my wife." This time, he didn't shrug. He stared at her in a kind of steady demand that made her…restless. "And I will act accordingly, of course."

Amelia felt as if she'd cinched herself into something horribly tight. For a moment she wasn't sure she could force a breath, and that restlessness made her itch. But she made herself stand still.

And she kept her voice cool. "I want to make sure we're both really clear about the fact that you're threatening me. With sex."

She thought that might slap at him. Offend him, at the very least.

But instead, Teo smiled in that edgy way that had been making her pulse jagged since she'd jolted awake to find him standing over her, taking over her field of vision. For a wild moment she hadn't been able to tell if she was asleep or awake.

There was no mistaking the fact she was awake now. He reached over and slid his hand over her hard, clenched jaw.

And then slowly, almost lazily, dragged his thumb over her lips.

Amelia felt as if she was the fire behind them, then. As if he'd stoked the flames—her—that easily, shaming her.

Or maybe she only *wanted* to be shamed. Because what she felt was a storm of sensation, galloping through her. Her nipples felt bright, hard. Her breasts were heavy. She felt something like chills running down her limbs, then sinking deep inside her until they formed a kind of tangle, too hot and too greedy down low in her belly.

"Do you feel threatened?" Teo asked her. Goading her. "Or do you feel something else entirely?"

"Everything you do is a threat," she managed to say. What she didn't do was pull away from him. "That's a natural consequence of kidnapping and abducting someone, I think you'll find."

But his hand was still on her face, and she could feel herself shaking, deep inside. Like the tectonic plates that kept her upright— that made her who she was—were shifting whether she liked it or not.

"I think you are trembling, *cariña*. I think you are terribly, surpassingly hungry." And somehow she couldn't pretend, even to herself, that he was talking about food. "Hot and wet, are you not?"

"Of course not." Her voice was barely more than a whisper.

"Here's another choice," he said, all that edge and quiet insinuation. "I'll make it easy for you. No need to declare yourself too openly, in a way you will not be able to take back. No need to remind us both too closely of that night back in September. All you have to do is stay exactly where you are."

He didn't elaborate on what would happen if she did that. He didn't have to.

"...or?"

"Or you can go into the kitchen and find a different way to please me." One arrogant brow lifted. "I prefer to start my days with a hot fire and a small *desayuno*, which I keep far simpler than you Americans are wont to do. No platters of dessert masquerading as breakfast foods." That brow seemed to arch even more intensely. "A *café con leche*, please."

He said *please*. Amelia heard him. But she wasn't foolish enough—yet—to imagine that was anything but an order.

And there was only one choice, obviously. No matter what he seemed to think. There was only one possible choice—and yet, for a terrifying moment that seemed to stretch on into eternity, she wavered.

Amelia stood there, gazing up at him, wondering if she could truly read that austere face of his or if she only wished she could.

Wondering what would happen if she let herself melt the way she wanted to do.

Wondering too many things that she should have known better than to allow into her head in the light of day, when wondering what it would be like to indulge herself with this man was what had gotten her into this position in the first place.

*Pull yourself together,* she snapped at herself. *Now.*

She didn't only step back, then. She jolted away from him and around him, wrenching herself out of the way of too much temptation.

Because worse by far than the molten heat between her legs was the ache in her chest.

Amelia blinked back the unexpected moisture in her eyes as she tried to find her way around the small kitchen. The deep sink basin boasted a pump in place of a faucet, and the water that poured out was clear and fresh. And even as her body shuddered through leftover reactions—to Teo, to this situation she found herself in, to her own body's betrayal of her—she tried to focus on the task at hand.

Outside the window a pretty winter sun peeked over the frozen slopes of the surrounding peaks. They were clearly very high up—and Amelia clung to the altitude as an explanation for why she felt so dizzy. It was the height, not the man. Clearly.

And it was almost helpful, really, to have something odd and a little overwhelming to do, like become a rustic barista in an ancient cabin, on command. But then, that was the part of her unconventional life with her mother that she liked best. Amelia had always done well thinking on her feet, and making herself into whoever and whatever the moment required.

The pumped-in water was ice cold, and she filled a small bucket and then brought it to the open pot over the fire. Then she set about building up the fire below.

She'd assumed that this was the kind of absurd task that featured in the kinds of reality shows she liked to watch to relax, and so was pleasantly surprised when she found ground espresso in the stocked cupboards, and better still, a classic silver stovetop espresso maker to put it in. She ladled water out of the pot, then put the espresso maker on the grate.

And when she turned to see if Teo was watching her come to grips with his medieval kitchen, she found that simmering black gaze steady on her in a way that made her chest ache. Again.

She reminded herself it was the altitude.

"Is this what hereditary dukes do for fun?" she asked. Perhaps more archly than the average servant might. "Take themselves off into the mountains and pretend to be one with the common folk? I'm assuming it didn't occur to you that us common folk like electricity and gas mains these days, just like you people in your big houses?"

"I prefer my servants to express their deference in silence," he said, sounding deep and mysterious, like a brick wall of privilege and that damnable sensuality she wished—oh, how she wished—didn't get into her veins like that.

"Then you should have kidnapped a better class of personal maid," she shot back.

But she was the one who turned away again, unable somehow to hold that stare of his.

When the espresso was finally bubbling, she poured it into a cup, added milk and delivered it. And then felt that itchy restlessness sweep over her again. More acutely this time.

"Now what?" And, yes, her voice was belligerent. Her body language matched it. "I've waited on you. Is that really what you want?"

Teo took his time lifting his cup. He took his time tasting the *café con leche* he'd asked for, until Amelia started fidgeting with the need to slap it out of his hand—

"Ordinarily I would say that you should go directly into cleaning, as this floor is appallingly dirty." Teo's gaze raked over her in a way she might have thought was dispassionate had she not been standing so close to him. Close enough to see the gleam in those black eyes. "But I am ever mindful that no matter the choices you made, and no matter my feelings about them, you are carrying my heir. I will therefore allow you an hour to yourself. I suggest you clean yourself up. Eat something. And then reapply yourself to the task at hand—and with a pleasant demeanor more suited to your role, please."

"I have no intention of getting naked in a tiny, remote cabin with a man who feels justified in holding me prisoner and making me his own, personal Cinderella, thank you."

Of course, the moment she said the word *naked*, all she could picture was Teo naked. It made her head spin all the more.

"If you do not do as I ask, I will take it as an invitation to do as I wish," Teo replied, his attention on the coffee she'd made him as if he was making offhanded remarks instead of threats.

Threats she fully believed he would carry out.

And for once in her life, Amelia decided that the smart move was to keep her mouth shut. Discretion was the better part of valor, or so she'd read once in school.

Maybe being trapped on the top of the mountain with a brooding, uncompromising duke who had it in for her—and who might very well take what he wanted, with her body's enthusiastic consent, a possibility that horrified her even as it made her belly quiver with longing—was an excellent place to discover if that were true.

The days took on their own, unique shape.

Amelia slept on the couch by the fire, and though she didn't strip down to the T-shirt she normally preferred to sleep in, she found that it wasn't necessary to keep herself fully dressed, either. Teo made no further attempts to put his hands on her.

She told herself that made her riotously glad.

The cold, careful light woke her in the early mornings. She built the fire back up, then started the water boiling. In the first few days there, she'd wondered how far he was going to take it. Would he send her out into the wilderness in some attempt to rustle up food from the snow and ice? Would he make her scrub the floors with a toothbrush, like some kind of Catholic school nun?

But she should have known that even Teo at his most rustic was far too sophisticated—or pampered—to leave himself victim to the vagaries of either nature or Amelia's hesitant servitude. The cabin was well stocked. The cupboards were filled with dry goods and she quickly discovered that there was also a cold chest that had been conveniently filled.

Amelia got to indulge her self-righteous indignation at his high-handedness and arrogance every time she served him, as ordered. And better still, she secretly got to indulge every last domestic urge she'd ever had, but had never had the occasion to entertain. Because Marie French did not lower herself to domestic chores. She had raised Amelia to disdain anything that smacked of what she called *chambermaiding.*

*A smart girl aspires to run the house, not clean it,* she always said.

But Amelia quite enjoyed a good clean. It was satisfying. It was a clear, indisputable accomplishment. And maybe it also felt a bit like penance, for deceiving Teo in the first place—something she would die before she admitted out loud.

While the water warmed in the mornings, she liked to go outside—wrapped up tight against the cold—and breathe in the frigid air. There was nothing in any direction save snow-covered inclines, the winter sky and, not long after she rose each morning on clear days, the full, glorious sunrise.

"Looking for your escape route?" Teo asked on one of those mornings, coming out to stand behind her there in the small clearing that she liked to think of as their yard. "It's a long walk down."

And she'd only looked over her shoulder at him, hoping she looked enigmatic, because she hadn't been thinking about walking down at all. She'd been thinking about staying here forever, happily cut off—cut free—from the noise and hustle of her life.

Winter days were short, and sometimes the sun never rose at all. It was all snow and storm, howling winds, and the days bled one into the next, dark outside and bright within.

As the days passed, Amelia found her shoulders seemed to drop from their usual place up at her ears. She found herself holding her breath less as she bustled around, oddly delighted that the tasks before her were simple and easily executed. Cleaning a floor was a far more appealing prospect than untangling her mother's money issues. Sweeping or dusting felt like a holiday compared with the usual long, torturous phone calls in which her mother would tell her things no daughter wanted to know, usually involving sex. Amelia had never been much of a cook, but it was only possible to produce simple things here, so that was what she did. She didn't have to worry about whether or not her culinary attempts were good, only that they were edible.

And that, too, was infinitely preferable to presenting herself as her mother's escort of an evening, subject to Marie's cheerful critique of her clothes, her hair, even the expression she wore on her face. Not to mention the running commentary on how Amelia ought to have been living her life.

Teo, meanwhile, was remarkably…easygoing. In comparison.

Well. Perhaps that wasn't the right word.

He didn't critique her, but he watched her. She would look up from some menial task or other to find him studying her, that stern mouth of his unsmiling and whole worlds in his eyes that she couldn't quite read.

Teo made her heart stutter in her chest, and she found herself in a constant state of awareness. She always knew exactly where he was, and when he went off on his hikes the cabin felt strange and almost too large without him.

One night, after they'd eaten the simple dinner she'd made—that he insisted she serve, then eat with him—she went to rise and clear the plates as usual, but he stopped her.

"It has been ten days," he said, and it occurred to her with a jolt that she'd stopped counting. What did that say about her? "I expected far more complaints."

"Are you asking for a list of complaints? Or bemoaning the fact that I haven't offered any?"

"If you think you can wait me out, you should know that you can't." His voice was blunt, that gaze direct. "I told you already. I come from a timeless bloodline. Ten days, ten months. It is all the same to me."

"I'm afraid it won't be the same, actually," she said drily. "Because unless you plan to hand deliver this child yourself, there's a very specific time limit to how long you can keep me here."

He made a soft noise that was not quite a laugh. "Do you imagine me incapable of flying in a medical team?"

"Threat, threat, threat," she said lightly, mocking him. "You gave me a choice, Teo. I took it. It's not my fault if you're rethinking that now."

To her surprise, his mouth curved. "*Cariña*, I am not the one who wakes in the night, gasping for air."

He couldn't possibly know what she dreamed about. Amelia told herself that, fiercely and repeatedly. *He couldn't know.* He could have no idea that she woke up flushed so hot she had to toss off her blankets though the room was always cold. That her thighs ached, her breasts hurt, and between her legs, she burned.

Oh, how she burned.

He couldn't know any of those things. He thought she was gasping for air, not gasping his name.

But as she gazed at him, and the way he lounged there like the Duke of impeccable lineage he was, the faintest trickle of what she told herself was horror snuck down her spine. It had to be horror, and not any of the other things that swirled around inside her, daring her to look at them straight.

"What do you get out of this?" she asked him.

Or, really, threw out there into all that "horror" that danced between them as surely as the snowstorm howled about outside.

"You will have to be more specific," Teo replied.

"I can see the appeal of this place," Amelia said, more sternly than necessary. Because she was desperate, suddenly, and just as desperate not to show it. "It's so easy to forget that there's a whole world that doesn't live inside a mobile phone. There's something rewarding in stepping away from it all. Learning how to listen to the thoughts inside, for a change, instead of all that external noise."

All of that was true. But there was also him.

Teo, whom she had never managed to get over. Or past. Even the exorcism she'd thought she'd performed so brilliantly hadn't worked—even before she'd learned she was pregnant. She'd still woken up in the night, longing for him so hard she worried it might have physical repercussions. She'd wondered if her "stomach bug" was actually an extended reaction to having him and walking away from him.

She'd begun to think that she'd imprinted on him at too young of an age. That he'd stamped his mark on her, even though he hadn't liked her at all, and she was stuck with it.

Amelia certainly wouldn't want a lifetime of performing menial tasks and acting like a servant. But this felt...different. Like a gift, somehow. And she knew it wasn't the scrubbing. The polishing of this or that, however mindlessly meditative the task.

It was *him*.

It was breathing his air. It was looking up to find that gaze of his on her, because these days, he didn't look at her the way he had when she was a teenager. As if he couldn't fathom what such a lowly creature was doing in his life, invading his family. That was gone now. In this cabin, he looked at her the way a man looked at a woman.

That look heated her. Beguiled her. It made her head go funny and her legs feel wobbly, and she tried to pretend none of that was happening even as she tucked it away like a bit of treasure to hoard. Because there had been many years where all she'd ever wanted was Teo to see her. Really, truly *see* her, as a woman. And here, now, *finally*, he did.

And it only occurred to her while the question she'd asked him hung in the air that perhaps she was a little too invested in what Teo was getting out of this arrangement.

Amelia was old enough to know that a wise woman didn't go asking questions when she already knew that the answers could very well break her heart.

Or at least bruise it, significantly.

For the first time in almost ten full days, she found herself holding her breath.

"I enjoy my solitude," he said, and she got the impression that he chose those words carefully. Too carefully.

There was something in the way he sat there that was different, suddenly. Too tight, maybe. Coiled.

"How can it be solitude?" She tried to sound light and airy and wasn't at all sure she hit the mark. "You're not alone."

"Downgrading from a staff of hundreds to one is the next best thing," Teo said drily.

Amelia found herself studying her hands, but not looking at him didn't exactly help her. She could see him perfectly no matter if she was looking at him or not. He was like a brand on the inside of her eyelids. She felt like those kittens she'd read about in college, who spent their early lives behind bars, then saw bars forever whether they were caged or not.

And surely, if she was normal in any regard, she wouldn't find the notion of being caged by this man forever to be so…comforting.

He hated her. He might have been playing a waiting game here, but it was just another game. Why couldn't she remember that the way she should? He wanted to marry her and claim his child, but she would be very foolish indeed if she imagined that had anything to do with *her.* She knew better.

There was no reason at all that Teo de Luz should make her feel safe.

Especially not when he'd kidnapped her for the express purpose of bending her to his will—and she knew it. He'd been open about it.

"I'm delighted I make you feel like you're alone," she said, making her voice wry. Amused.

"On the contrary," he murmured, an edge she didn't quite understand in his voice. "I find it difficult to remember a time when you were not here."

"Did you come here often with your father?"

She blurted that out. Because there was that gleam in his gaze and a shuddering in response, deep inside her. And she could tell herself any number of truths, or try. But that was very different from telling them to him.

Teo's sensual lips twitched. "My father and I were not friends, Amelia. He did not encourage intimacies of that kind."

She nodded, too eagerly. "My mother always said that the tragedy of your father was that he wanted to feel, but couldn't."

Teo's gaze cooled dramatically, and Amelia froze, in direct response.

"Did she indeed? What other insights did your mother have to share about her blessedly brief time as the Duchess of Marinceli, pray tell?"

And frozen or not, there would never be a better opportunity for her to say things to him that she had never dared speak aloud when she was younger. Things she hadn't even said when she'd come to find him in that palace of his.

Things she knew he had no interest in hearing. Ever.

"You've never understood my mother," she said, briskly. "All you see is the surface.

Too blonde. Too comfortable showing off her body. All flash, no substance. Though I'm certain you use different words."

"I prefer not to discuss your mother at all."

"It's easier to talk about her than it is to understand her," Amelia said, staunchly. "She'd be the first person to say that it's just as easy to fall in love with a rich man as a poor one, but the key point is, she actually does fall in love."

For a moment it was as if the storm outside had breached the walls, the howling was so intense. But in the next moment she realized that was nothing more than the noise inside her.

Teo looked about as approachable as a slab of granite. "If you are about to launch into some kind of poetic rhapsody about the depths of your mother's heart, Amelia, I would beg you to rethink."

"It doesn't last, perhaps, but when she commits, she means it. She loved your father."

"She conned him," Teo said, his words distinct and a kick of menace beneath them. "He made a fool of himself over that woman."

"She has that effect," Amelia said softly. "But that doesn't mean it wasn't real. It was.

I understand that all you can see is what it meant to your bloodline. Your title. Your—"

"My *family*, Amelia," he belted at her. "My bloody *family*."

That sliced through Amelia like the vicious winter wind outside. She lost her breath, staring across at him while an expression she'd never before seen on his face twisted him up.

His eyes blazed. But this time with a kind of torment.

"My parents used to tell me stories about their great luck," Teo bit out, still lounging there, though there wasn't a single part of him that wasn't tense and coiled to spring. She could see it with her own eyes. "Because their marriage, while not technically arranged, might as well have been. Their parents chose them for one another when they were small. But they were lucky, they said, because they liked each other. Loved each other, even. And in a family like mine, that is never a prerequisite for a long marriage."

Suddenly, this cage of hers seemed tighter all around her. But Teo was still talking.

"When she died, I expected my father to mourn. Instead, he dated." And the way he said that word was like a slap. "I understand a man has needs, even if I would prefer not to think of my father's. And I resigned myself to these things because it was his personal business. Not mine. Who cared how many women he squired about? He had been married for a long time. The line of succession was secured. Why shouldn't he sow some oats, if he was so inclined?"

Amelia didn't really think that was a question. Certainly not one that required an answer from her. Especially not when his expression was so harsh.

"But then he met your mother," Teo said darkly. "And he was not content with sowing, or squiring. He fell in love."

"A fate worse than death," Amelia murmured.

His gaze seemed to blaze even hotter when that should not have been possible. "He loved her. And she left him. And he grieved your mother, not mine. He engaged on a downward spiral of inappropriate lovers, drink and despair. I believe that led to his death five years ago. And no, I do not forgive her."

Amelia told herself to bite her tongue. She meant to. But she couldn't.

"I think you mean you couldn't forgive *him*," she said softly.

And she watched Teo…implode.

He didn't move. He didn't shake or roll his eyes in the back of his head, or anything so dramatic. But still, she could see it. The bomb, the burn.

His eyes blazed. And then he seemed nothing so much as haunted.

And she felt her heart lurch painfully in her chest.

For a long, endless sort of moment that could have been years, ages, millennia, she stayed where she was. Suspended in Teo's gaze, where ghosts lurked, and beneath it, she saw a different version of the ruthless, uncompromising Duke.

A son who had lost a mother, then a father— the latter some time before his death.

Amelia had wanted so badly for Teo to see her all these years. Why hadn't she realized how little *she* saw *him*?

The wind howled outside. A log collapsed in the fire.

"I suggest you clean up," he said, his voice too quiet. It rang in her like condemnation, making her fight to restrain a sob. "And you should know that you have ash on your face. Soot, perhaps."

And at another time, maybe, that would have embarrassed her. How long had it been there? Had he ever planned to tell her? But tonight those questions hardly seemed to matter. Amelia lifted her hand and rubbed at her cheek, not surprised when her fingers came away smudged black.

"Better soot than sorrow," she replied.

And she didn't see him move. It was a kind of blur of ferocity and grief, a new take on that same old hunger they'd been dancing around for too long now.

One moment he was sitting opposite her. The next, he was hauling her up to her feet and then holding her there, his big hands wrapped around her shoulders.

"My servants do not talk to me of sorrow," he gritted out at her. "And they do not presume to mention my esteemed, late and much lamented father. Do you understand me? Either know your place or change it, Amelia. Those are your only choices."

His hands clenched tighter, digging into her skin—but in a way that made her whole body ignite. The fire in the grate paled next to the flames that danced between them, brighter and hotter by the second.

And she was sure that he would pull her close, then take her mouth—

But he didn't.

Teo let her go. Then he turned on his heel and strode from the room.

Leaving her there alone as the winter wind battered at the walls.

Amelia told herself she'd won. She was the victor. But she looked down at her hand, and wondered why she felt as if all of her was ash, instead.

# CHAPTER EIGHT

AMELIA STOOD WHERE he'd left her for a long while.

Slowly, she sank back down onto the sofa behind her, not sure whether she chose to sit or was forced to because her knees no longer functioned properly.

She kept staring at her hand and without entirely meaning to, found herself rubbing her fingers together, transferring the dark soot from one finger to the next. From one hand to the next.

And no matter how long she sat there, no matter how still she held herself, she couldn't seem to catch her breath.

She felt all the usual things she always did when she was in the presence of Teo. Frustrated desire, as ever. The driving need to impress him, somehow. That greedy, voracious thing in her that *wanted*—wanted anything he would give her and hundreds of things he never had. Not entirely.

But underneath it all, she felt a funny, new knot in her gut that she was terribly afraid was shame.

Because through all of this, since she was a teenager and on into her adulthood, she'd thought about Teo far too much. She'd thought about him. Dreamed about him. Found him unaccountably stuck between her and any attempt she made to transfer this hunger to someone else. She'd raged about him. Cried about him. Made vows to stop fixating on him and then, finally, she'd come up with a plan to exorcise him.

But had she ever really thought of him as a man? A whole person?

She knew she hadn't. He was her stepbrother. The Duke's son. Then the Duke himself. He was a hundred titles and had a thousand names, many she'd made up purely to entertain herself, especially when she'd been sixteen.

But she'd never thought of him as just a man back then. Or since. As a complicated, layered person.

In her fantasies, whether he'd been good

or evil or something altogether else, she had never thought of him like that.

Like her.

The reason she'd concealed her appearance at the Masquerade wasn't because she'd worried that sleeping with her would cause him to have any kind of feelings. It had never occurred to her that Teo had any feelings. Not really. Not unless they were acrid and accusatory, or tangled up somehow in his title.

She'd told herself it was because he wouldn't let her close to him if he knew who she was. And that was a part of it, certainly.

But she'd always imagined that if anyone *could* see her, truly, it would be Teo. And when it came down to it, she'd wanted to make sure he didn't.

Just as he hadn't wished her to see the real part of him tonight.

Almost as if they were similar, after all.

And it was a strange and comprehensive sort of shattering, then, that took her over. That broke her apart into shards of guilt and shame alike, and something else. Something that she couldn't quite name, but knew had to do with the things they had in common.

Far more than the enormous gulf between a commoner and a duke.

Because the notion that Teo might be no more than flesh and blood, perfectly capable of feeling every last thing that she did made her...hurt.

More than simply *hurt*.

It pounded in her temples and turned her stomach like too much wine. It tangled around itself, like a thick and braided thing.

And still, that scalding heat seemed to lick her, head to toe.

She rose again, and she didn't bother to wash the ash and soot from her hands. She'd crossed this room a thousand times since they'd arrived, but tonight it seemed to take on marathon proportions. Miles upon miles, she was sure, and then she was at the door to the bedroom.

She pushed it open, her hand flat against the door, dimly aware that she was leaving her handprint behind—one more thing it would fall to her to clean in the morning. Her throat was so dry she was surprised it didn't turn into its own kindling, and her eyes were glassy, almost foggy.

But that didn't in any way prevent her gaze from cutting straight to Teo.

And staying there while her heart leaped.

The bedroom was deceptively simple because it was dominated by the bed at the far wall that offered a stunning view out over the Pyrenees. She had cleaned in here defiantly, certain that he expected her to balk, and she'd been unable to avoid thinking about what it would look like from the bed. A person could wake up of a morning and watch that very sunrise that she stepped outside to look at every day.

Or a person could concentrate on what was in the bed, instead.

Teo was sprawled there as if he'd seen all those dreams she kept having after all, and was trying to reenact them in the soft light from the lanterns. His dark gaze was unreadable, and stormier than usual. And it was something, wasn't it, to know that she was responsible for introducing all that thunder to his gaze tonight.

She wanted to feel that as a victory, but she didn't. She couldn't.

And Amelia couldn't keep her eyes on his face. Not when he had bared the whole of his chest to her view, which should have made him seem smaller, like any naked thing.

But Teo looked…bigger. An immensity in human form, as if the trappings of his title and general magnificence were mere props to distract the unwary from the truth of him. He was golden and beautiful, like the sort of sculpture he would collect to display in his gallery and scholars would flock to, to fawn over.

She felt a bit like fawning herself, and all he was doing was sitting up against the headboard, a book at his side that he'd clearly tossed aside when the door had opened.

And even at the Masquerade, she had only seen him clothed. She had never gotten to look at all his smooth, toned flesh stretched across muscle and bone.

It was like staring into the sun.

She was afraid that if she kept it up, she would go blind.

And yet she couldn't seem to make herself stop.

"Let me guess what I've done to merit a personal visit," Teo said, and his voice held all that thunder, all the storms she could see with her own eyes. "Have you had an attack of conscience, Amelia?"

"Of course not," she said, trying to sound certain as she stood there, half in and half out of the bedroom. "The truth might be uncomfortable, but it doesn't require the intervention of conscience…depending on your truth, I suppose."

"Are we telling truths tonight?" And there was a warning in that voice of his. Something dangerous wrapped up in silk and heat. A wise woman would walk away. Amelia stayed where she was. "Perhaps you can explain to me why you've taken so easily to a life of drudgery."

She swallowed, because that cut a bit. It stung. "Not a life. Just a little while. You can do anything if it's temporary."

An odd look moved over his beautiful face. "I wouldn't know."

And he wouldn't. Of course he wouldn't. There wasn't a single thing about the life of a member of the de Luz family that was *temporary*. Everything was stone and consequence, handed down throughout time and stretching far off into the future.

*A prison is a prison,* he'd told her. *It is up to you how you would like to serve your time.*

Why had she never stopped to think how those words applied to him, too?

"I do not think it is the temporary aspect that you like," he continued, in that same dangerous way. "I think it is quite the contrary. You imagine yourself in a place like this. It is a small cabin, but sturdy, and has stood right here in one form or another for centuries. You are thirsty for that kind of connection, are you not?"

Her throat hurt, it was so dry. "I'm not thirsty for anything."

"I am not the only one who grieves," Teo said, as inevitable as thunder. As terrible as the storm outside. And in here, too. "But you lost something rather different, did you not? The whole of your childhood."

She had wanted to be seen. By him, specifically. And now she wanted to hide.

But there was ash on her hands and that aching thing where her heart should have been. And she was the one who had hidden herself last fall. She was the one who had made all of this happen. She owed him the penance she'd been paying.

And that likely meant it wasn't up to her to dictate the terms of that penance. Even if this was the price she had to pay.

"I had a marvelous childhood," Amelia retorted, a knee-jerk response that seemed to roll up and out of her whether she liked it or not. Because it was one thing to think about penance and scrub a not very dirty floor. It was something else entirely to pry herself open and expose herself to him. To anyone, but especially to him. "My mother took me everywhere with her."

"Like a pet."

"Like a *friend*."

"Parents are not meant to be friends," Teo said with soft menace. "One cannot parent one's friend. And children are by definition in want of a parent. I think you will find that it is all right there in the titles. Parent. Child. Friend. Not the same, is it?"

Amelia made herself laugh, trying for airy and bright—but what came out made his dark brow lift.

"Not everyone was raised up into a glorious bloodline, filled with tedious history and mausoleums with their names chiseled into the stone at birth," she said. "Some people prefer a more carefree existence."

Her childhood had been many things, none of them *carefree*. And Amelia couldn't understand why she felt one thing and then opened her mouth to find something else entirely coming out. As if her tongue was more afraid of vulnerability than she was.

And meanwhile, Teo lounged in that bed half-naked, like some kind of god. Or satyr. And whatever he was, he made her dizzy.

She wanted to fall down all over him, and burn herself on all that smooth, hard male perfection.

The way she had last fall, but with all of her, this time. All of him.

But she couldn't seem to make her body move. Her legs were planted into the floor, as if her feet had taken root.

Because if she went to him like this, without the mask or the dress, the lipstick or the red hair, she would be wide open. Exposed.

He would know how much she wanted him.

How much she always had.

"You might convince me that your mother loved my father, in time," Teo said darkly, that gaze of his too hot. "You might even convince me that your mother is not the gold digger she seems, but a woman who cannot help but fall in love. Repeatedly. And only upward on the social ladder. But you will never convince me that Marie French loves anything so much as she loves herself. Not even you, Amelia."

It wasn't as if Amelia hadn't heard such things before. Or some variation thereof. But she had never heard it quite like this.

Quietly.

With that devastating certainty that rolled through her like truth.

The truth she had never wanted to look at face-on.

Something walloped her, and she wanted to tip back her head and let it out. Sob through it. Scream about it. Just get it out—

But almost before she could process the hit of it, something else smacked her down.

Because she didn't think that Teo was being cruel for the sake of it.

He was lying there, naked to the waist—and for all she knew, naked beneath that sheet—and he was looking at her as if he could see deep inside her. To the place where that great sob remained trapped. To the place where she'd hidden from everything and everyone for as long as she could remember.

Even him, last fall.

But here, in this cabin on top of a remote mountain in the Pyrenees, he saw her.

Just as she'd wanted. Just as she'd feared. *He saw her.*

Amelia had a brief thought for that sixteen-year-old version of herself, who would have done anything to gain his notice. Anything at all. No matter what it took, no matter the cost. And now she understood things she couldn't have, then. That some prices hurt to pay almost beyond bearing, because the way he looked at her was ruthless. Pitiless. Merciless, even.

It wasn't in any way the kind of longing looks she'd imagined in her youth.

But it was perfect.

Scathing, serious, beautiful and perfect.

And Amelia still couldn't look away.

"Much as I enjoy watching you squirm in my doorway, with soot on your face and ash prints on my walls," Teo said, "this is not what I would consider an ideal way to end a trying evening."

He lifted that brow of his, an arrogant query that on a face like his was more properly a demand. And some part of her was amazed that he could seem just as untouchable, just as remote and powerful, lying down half-naked in a bed as he did when he was standing—likely surrounded by portraiture and statuary, all of them bearing features that looked like his and taken together, told the story of Spain.

"What is it you want?" he asked, holding her gaze hostage.

For once in her life, Amelia didn't dare look away. She didn't dare hide.

She felt torn asunder, though she knew she stood in one piece. She had spent the whole of her life trying her best to pretend a great number of things. That her mother loved her the way a mother should. That her life was a madcap adventure.

That this man did not matter to her. Because he shouldn't have.

Amelia had tried to forget him. And when that didn't work, she'd tried a spot of immersion therapy.

And here she was again, and it was worse this time. She carried his child. His son. The heir to that absurd monster of a house.

Amelia knew that he would never allow her to take their son away from him. That he would not have allowed it if the only thing he planned to leave his heir was debt. Perhaps she'd known that before she'd gotten on that plane in San Francisco. Perhaps she'd always known it.

She could pretend all she liked that if she was stubborn enough, dedicated enough to this penitent game she was playing, he would give in—but she knew better, didn't she?

The Duke did not give. He did not bend. There was not one part of his life that required compromise or quarter, and accordingly, he offered neither. He never would.

And suddenly Amelia felt as exhausted as if she'd crawled up that winding mountain road on her own hands and knees. She felt as if he'd clawed away a crucial veil she kept between her and the reality of her life, of her, of what she'd done to both of them, and it hurt.

It all hurt.

Maybe it had always hurt, and she was only now admitting it.

Her hands crept over her belly, and she thought about longevity. About centuries upon centuries of one family, one house, one enduring vision that united them all.

And how, in comparison, the ragtag itinerant lifestyle she'd lived with her mother seemed so shoddy.

If she could choose a life for her baby—and she could, by God, and would—she would not choose hers.

All she had to do was surrender.

And risk that he would see the real truth about her stamped all over her face, her body. That without her various masks, he would know the real her.

And scarier still, her heart.

"I will ask again," he said, his voice more stern, if such a thing was possible. All ice and disapproval, and she was a twisted creature, wasn't she, that she craved that from him. It made her restless, hot. "What do you want? Why did you come in here?"

"I'm ready," she said, and had the sense that she'd run to the edge of one of the mountain cliffs all around and instead of stopping, had catapulted herself out into the great abyss.

Now came the fall.

And if she was very, very lucky, a little bit of something like flight on the way down.

"Are you indeed." He considered her while her heart hurt and between her legs, she was bright and needy. "Ready for what, *cariña*?"

"I'm ready…"

And she couldn't bring herself to say it all. He wanted a wife. A duchess. It didn't mean he wanted her. Though at the same time, she knew the ways he did want her. She could feel them all, a molten thing inside her.

She wanted those things, too.

She wanted everything.

And she had to imagine that if she gave him what he wanted, someday—some way, as she marched along this road that had been carved out for her by Marinceli brides for hundreds and hundreds of years, because love was not a prerequisite for a duke of his magnificence— she would convince him to give her what she wanted, too.

All the things she wanted.

She cleared her throat, because it was still so dry she was surprised it didn't catch flame. But the rest of her was taking care of that. She was surprised she wasn't burnt straight down to a cinder.

"I'm ready," she said. And found herself smiling, almost despite herself, because a Pyrrhic victory was still better than a total loss. It had to be. "Are you going to share that bed?"

# CHAPTER NINE

TEO TRIED TO tell himself that passion was not the point here, that this had been an exercise in obedience only, but his body was paying him no mind. He was hard and ready, on the verge of desperate—the way he'd been since she'd strolled back into his life.

Amelia stayed in the doorway for another moment, as if she was hesitating. Waiting, he realized. For him to answer her question.

It was hard for him to imagine she couldn't see his answer, stamped all over him.

The past ten days had been torture. Sheer and utter torture, that he'd had to pretend didn't affect him at all. Amelia had bustled about playing house, which hadn't been why he'd brought her here. Quite the opposite, in fact. He'd assumed that a woman like her—a woman like her mother, more properly— would be unable to last twenty-four hours pretending to be a servant. He been certain they'd be back home and planning their wedding, and their future, within two days' time at the most.

Amelia was nothing like he'd expected.

He had actually spoken to her about his father's besottedness with Marie, something he had never really discussed with anyone because it was too easy, from there, to delve into his own sense of loss over his mother. And how his father's obvious obsession with another woman had seemed to Teo like he was making a mockery of not only Teo's grief, but of his first marriage altogether.

How had he even started down this road with Amelia?

He didn't understand how he could have been so wrong about her. Assuming he was actually wrong, that was. Assuming this wasn't simply some game she was playing.

But he thought not. Not when her remarkable eyes were so big and bright. Not when her lips parted as if her breath was its own kind of torture—a sensation he knew too well just then. And not when she'd left a perfect handprint of ash on his door.

"By all means," he said, fighting to sound appropriately unaffected when really, he wanted to leap from the bed and charge her like an untried boy. "Join me."

He waited.

And still, she hesitated, there on the threshold with something too raw to be hope in her gaze and soot on her cheek.

"Let us be clear about what it means if you climb into this bed with me," he found himself saying, every muscle in his body clenched tight in anticipation. Need. And a driving force he wanted to call rage. Though he knew better. "What it means if you take this step."

He was afraid he knew exactly what it was, and it wasn't rage.

"I know," Amelia said softly. "Believe me, Teo. I know."

For a moment that he was certain lasted a thousand years or more, their gazes clashed. Held. And he could see something in the violet depths that made him shake.

It threw him. It humbled him. It made him feel as if he was soaring.

All at once.

But before he could catalog it, process it, compartmentalize it and move to counter it, somehow, she began to move.

She wore her usual uniform, which would

never have passed muster if she was an actual servant in a grand house. She liked stretchy pants that clung lovingly to her thighs, her calves, and layered-on distractingly soft T-shirts and that finely woven sweater that she'd worn the first day. And since.

There wasn't a single part of her that was appropriate. From the ash on her face to her bare feet, where her toenail polish was bright red and chipped.

Teo had been used to the best of everything, all of his life. He had never understood until these past ten days how limiting that was. And all the glorious, mesmerizing things it left out of the equation.

Like the way Amelia frowned so fiercely as she slept, and how flushed her cheeks were when she first woke in the mornings. The soft little noises she made, of delight or frustration, as she found her way through the various chores he'd set for her. How her blond hair looked when she knotted it carelessly on the top of her head, and the little curls that sprang up at her nape when she worked over the fire.

Ten days ago he would have sworn up and down that his baser urges aside, he could only ever view a woman like this is as a convenience, or temporary fix. His tastes were too refined, too deeply aristocratic, to seek permanence with so little effort toward outward perfection.

But that was before he'd spent ten days battling his own intense urges when it came to this woman.

There was nothing perfect about her. And yet somehow, every imperfection he found made him want her more.

Her face without makeup. That crooked smile she wore when he lapsed off into some history lesson she hadn't requested. The look of wonder and hope on her face when he caught her with her hands on her belly.

More and more and more. Teo was full up on *more*, but it didn't stop. It only got worse.

Amelia came to the side of the bed, then lifted one knee to slide it onto the mattress, slowly. As if she still wasn't certain about what she was doing.

Meanwhile, Teo was so greedy for her he thought he might burst into flame. Or perhaps he already had.

"There's no going back," he warned her, his voice gruff. "If you choose this, it is done. We will marry. And soon. The legitimacy of the Marinceli heir can never be in question."

"Must you threaten me even now?" she asked, and though her violet gaze was intense, he thought her smile was real. And that shook him, too. "Is this a duke thing? Or just a you thing?"

"I want to make sure this is an informed decision on your part," he said, dark and low because it was all he could manage. "Because once the decision is made it is permanent."

"Why are you acting as if I have a choice now?"

She pulled her other leg onto the bed with her, so she was kneeling there at his side. And her bougainvillea eyes were alive with heat and laughter. And he, who had been surrounded by interchangeably lovely things for the whole of his life, had never glimpsed anything as beautiful as this.

Amelia beside him, her eyes bright and laughter like a new flush on her face.

*Like hope,* he thought, and that made something in him lurch.

"I am prepared to wait here as long as it takes," he said, even darker and more gruff, to cover that lurch inside him where he should have felt nothing at all. "Once it is done, it is done."

"Your Excellency," she said, and he could

hear the laughter then, too, "do you ever shut up?"

And there was no time to take umbrage at that impertinence, because she simply… toppled forward, flinging herself across his chest with a thud.

Teo had never thought of himself as a man of extremes, because there weren't any in his life. Marincelis endured. The centuries passed. Extremes came and went, like little pops of color and moments of theater, but there was always the dukedom. Unchangeable and eternal.

But Amelia was a tangle of too much color to wave away. A snarled, hopeless knot. There was something profoundly silly in the way she flung herself against him, and he was not a silly man. She made him wish he was.

Amelia was touching him, then. He could feel the sweet weight of her breasts and felt it as her nipples turned to hard points against his chest.

And Teo had never felt this strange mixture of heat and laughter, silliness and that punch of sensuality that was all Amelia. Only Amelia. He felt almost breathless. Altered.

She lifted her head and grinned. When he

frowned, she grinned more. So he frowned all the harder.

Only after he did so did he realize he *wanted* to see her grin as she did then. Big. Bright. Fearless and beautiful.

"A good duchess does not tell her Duke to shut up, *cariña*," he said frostily. Though he couldn't maintain the tone. Not with her soft weight in his arms.

"You didn't say I had to be a good duchess," she said, laughing at him in that way only she dared. "Only that I had to become one. If you're expecting me to excel in the position, you should resign yourself to disappointment here and now."

But all Teo could think about then, like a flash of heat, was that he could no longer imagine anyone else in the role. Only her. Only Amelia, with soot on her face like an urchin, too loud and too inappropriate, and as of this moment, his.

Entirely his.

And with that, he was done waiting. Or playing Cinderella games.

He wrapped a palm around the nape of her neck, then drew her mouth to his.

And finally, the Nineteenth Duke of Marinceli claimed his Duchess.

\* \* \*

His mouth was all demand, delirious and divine in turn.

Any power Amelia might have imagined she was claiming by throwing herself on top of him—something she probably wouldn't have done if she thought it through—shifted in an instant. She still lay there on top of him, but he was the one in delicious control.

He held her head where he wanted it and he took her mouth with a lazy certainty that rolled into her, then through her, like a wildfire.

Every time he angled his head, every time he took the kiss deeper, the fire burned hotter.

And she felt delicate, and sacred, and something far earthier than either as he pulled her more tightly into his arms. The shift made her legs spread as she sprawled over him, and his hard thigh was *right there* where she was so soft and so hot.

It made her head spin.

Then again, it was hard to say which particular sensation was making her head spin.

And then her head was the least of her concerns, because he shifted again. She'd been paying attention to his hand at the nape of her neck, but it was the other one that got her attention then. His fingers splayed out over her bottom, and found their way beneath the hem of her shirt and sweater to find her bare skin.

Amelia had enjoyed two previous encounters with this man. At the Masquerade there had been the wild pleasure in that hallway, followed by what had happened in that salon after. And then there had been the morning she'd come to Spain to tell him about her pregnancy.

Both times she'd been fully dressed throughout.

She was dressed now, too. But the way his palm moved over the small of her back, then upward, she understood that she would not remain clothed for long. And the notion made her shudder.

In the next moment, he jackknifed up in the bed, taking her with him. He kept kissing her. Long, drugging kisses, so hot and intense, and in between each one he methodically rid her of her clothing with a certain skill that made her heart do cartwheels inside her. The sweater and the shirt he pulled off her in one go, and he easily removed the soft bra she wore. His big hands of his wrapped around her waist, then he tore his mouth from hers.

Amelia was dazed. Her lips felt swollen. She felt *glorious*, and she was half-naked, right there where he could see her.

The look in his dark gaze slammed through her, thick like greed.

Teo lifted her toward him, then took one hard, proud nipple in his mouth. And sucked.

And it was as if her head…flatlined. Except Amelia was fully aware of the sensation storming through her. Washing over her. Tossing her from one hot burst of flame into the next, brighter blaze.

There was so much…*skin*. He was hard in all the places she was soft, and the slide of her body against his elated her. *Tempted* her. She wanted to taste every inch of him. She wanted to rub herself against him, and see what happened. She didn't know what to do with her hands, so she put them everywhere. Anywhere.

He made a low noise that she remembered from before. It was so *male*. So deep and rumbly, and she could feel it like a new heat between her legs.

Then he slid one of those wicked hands around, slipping beneath the waistband of the stretchy trousers she wore, and again, it was as if her head blanked out.

Leaving her nothing but a mass of sensation and need, so intense it ate at her.

Then the whole world spun as he rolled them over. And this time, he found his way into her pants yet again, but from the front.

She remembered so vividly, there in the hall where he'd taken her that night last fall. The music and noise from the Masquerade had filled the hallway where they stood, his mouth on hers, and his clever, determined fingers tracing the slit in the side of her dress before making his way beneath it. And finding the center of her need. So easily.

Amelia almost shattered from the memory.

But reality was far better than any memory, because this time, instead of stroking her heat, he helped her strip the pants from her body. One leg then the next. She had the vague impression of his flat, ridged abdomen and his strong, hair-roughened thighs.

And the fact that he had been naked under that sheet, all this time, was like another bright flame.

Then they were naked. Together.

It felt like a storm.

She was in the storm, and he *was* the storm, and together, skin on skin, they were like thunder.

Teo plundered her mouth and Amelia died, again and again, but lived again to keep tasting him. Learning him. Losing herself in him, over and over again.

But then he was between her legs, the hardest part of him flush against her. Teo tipped his head back to meet her gaze, and she was keenly aware that she wore no mask this time. And neither did he.

Amelia was open and vulnerable and *herself* as he pressed against her, then into her. He was thick and big, and it was different, lying on her back on a bed.

She felt possessed. *Taken.* And it was so much better. So much hotter.

It took her a confused jumble of a moment to understand why.

"You're not…" But she had to stop and shudder when she felt him, lodged deep inside her body, filling her completely. "You're not wearing…"

He was propped up above her, his weight on his elbows and a fierce, intent look on his face. "No."

Her own breathing seemed too loud to her then, too wild. Too revealing.

And something clawed at her, some great sob or scream, or possibly it was panic. His chest was like a wall, and he surrounded her. He was *inside* her and he could *see* her, and the look on that austere face of his was pitiless.

But as she stared up at him, trying to catch her breath, trying to adjust to the size of him, he moved his hands to cup her face.

And Teo leaned his head down and pressed a soft kiss on her mouth.

It was a peck, really. But to Amelia, it felt like a poem.

The simplicity of it, the sweetness, pried open that tight little noose that had tightened around her. His thumbs moved against her jaw, she found air to breathe, and inside, she felt her body accept him.

And when this was over —when she felt like herself again—she would take the world to task for failing to mention that sex wasn't magically more comfortable when a person had only had it once before.

But here, now, Teo's gaze was black and intense. He was a hard length of steel deep inside her, almost too hot to bear. With no condom to dull the potency of his possession this time.

And her body had rolled straight from that would-be sob, that almost scream, into a delirious sort of desire. So intense she felt herself clamp down, and heard another growl from him as a reward.

So she did it again.

His mouth curved. "Okay?"

"Okay," she agreed, in a voice that sounded far too breathy and needy to be hers.

It felt like a chain between them. A set of vows like iron.

And that was when he began to move.

She remembered this part. That slick pull and thrust, that impossible rhythm. It was more than simply hot. He was so hard.

And it was different like this, with his weight and so much skin and his mouth against her neck.

She shattered at once, and then again. On and on he went, until she couldn't tell if she was shattering or recovering, climbing or falling.

It was all fire. Calamity and crisis, glory and need.

And this time, there was no one to hear them.

So he taught her how to scream. How to sob. How to cry out his name as she fell apart.

And when he took his own pleasure at last, he added his voice to the chorus and carried them both over that edge one more time.

She slept, hard and deep. And when she woke, it was still night. Teo was sprawled out beside her, one heavy arm anchoring her to his side.

The room was cool, but he was hot at her back.

It stunned her how safe that made her feel. How protected. When she had never slept in a bed with another person and had always imagined it would be strange, cluttered and uncomfortable.

The lantern still flickered beside the bed and when she turned beneath his arm, she watched it dance over his golden skin.

And she was somehow unsurprised when his eyes opened.

"You're awake," she said quietly. Foolishly.

The lantern light spun between them, all around them, and Amelia felt caught in it. Glued to him and lost in that dark gaze of his.

And she couldn't say she minded.

"We'll leave at first light," Teo said, but she didn't want to talk about that.

She didn't want to talk at all. She put her hand out and slid it over those sculpted, serious lips. And she smiled as his arrogant brows rose.

This time, she understood that the feeling expanding behind her ribs was as much a longing as it was lust. It was hope and fear entwined. But she didn't tell him that. She didn't intend to tell him any of that, ever.

Amelia crawled on top of him, smiled wickedly at him and then did exactly as she pleased. She tasted him. Everywhere.

By the time he flipped her over again, and rocketed them both toward that same bright finish, Amelia had convinced herself that she'd made the right choice. Because surely two people could not burn like this unless what fueled those flames was real.

*It had to be real.*

That was what she told herself the next morning, when Teo did exactly as promised and took her back to the historic seat of the Marinceli dukedom.

And set about making her his Duchess.

# CHAPTER TEN

"FAIRY TALES ARE for little girls," Marie said in that way of hers, half a throaty laugh and half an accusation. "Silly girls. Not grown women, Amelia."

If Amelia made it through her wedding without killing her mother, she thought it would be a miracle.

Teo had taken her back down from his mountain and put the rest of his plan into motion. Exactly as he told her he would.

"We will get married on the grounds of the estate," he told her as they flew out of the Pyrenees. He had boarded, disappeared into a stateroom and reappeared in a crisp suit. He had looked devastatingly attractive, of course, but Amelia had found herself mourning Teo in his jeans and a fisherman's sweater. "There's an ancient chapel that dates back to the Third Duke, which will suit our purposes."

By which he meant, his purposes. But Teo's purposes suited Amelia well enough.

Because this time, when she had her things sent from San Francisco and moved back into that same sprawling monstrosity of a house, it felt a whole lot more like a home. Because she got to share the ducal suite with Teo.

And while Teo was the remote, demanding Duke outside the doors to the bedroom suite, within them, he was hers.

There was not a single surface they did not explore. Not a single possibility they did not exploit for the greatest possible pleasure.

And she was so dizzy with the wonder of it in those first days after they came down from the mountain that she would have agreed to anything he asked. She was giddy, made of lust and delight, and it all seemed like a blur to her, looking back.

But reality had a way of intruding, even in the hushed halls of *el monstruo*. Teo gifted her a wardrobe she would have said she didn't want, particularly as he called it her "appropriate clothes," but he made it his business to compliment her so much when she wore what he'd chosen that she found herself reaching for his significantly more upscale selections. And when she was dressed in the sleek, quietly elegant clothes he liked, she found herself doing more with her hair. Wearing jewelry.

Becoming a duchess by default.

Teo also had his people confer with the appropriate authorities, produce the necessary documents—hers as well as his—and set a date for their wedding a week out. He further decreed it would be a simple affair.

"Just the two of us and the priest," he told her.

"You must be joking," she'd replied, sprawled out in cheerful abandon in his bed. Because that was where they always seemed to end up, on his side of the vast master suite that took up the better part of its own wing. "I can't get married without my mother."

"Whatever for?"

"She may be complicated," Amelia had admitted. "But she's my mother even so. She may love herself more than she does me—" And it should have bothered her, the way her voice cracked then. But his gaze was on her and she let her poor voice do as it would. "That is likely true. But that doesn't mean she doesn't love me deeply, you know."

"Your mother has already attended the wedding of one Duke of Marinceli," Teo had replied after a moment, sounding resigned. "Surely that is more than enough."

And if she wasn't hoarse from the way he'd just made her scream, and still a bit dizzy with it—not to mention the emotional wallop of considering Marie's selfishness all over again—Amelia might have taken offense at that.

"I promised that I would marry you," she'd reminded him instead. "I did not promise to marry you in secret, which would break my mother's heart forever."

Or dent it, anyway. Which to Amelia's mind was the same thing.

She thought that perhaps he was more affected by these things that went on between them, skin to skin, than he let on. Perhaps even as rocked as she was. Because all he did was sigh.

Amelia had taken that as assent.

But then she'd had to...tell her mother. Not only that she was pregnant, but that the father of her baby was, of all people, Teo de Luz. And more, that she was going to marry him and become the newest Duchess of Marinceli.

Soon.

The initial conversation had not gone well.

But now the wedding was in two days.

Marie had arrived in all her state the night before, dripping in conciliatory smiles to celebrate with her only child. And her former stepson, who had looked as if he was suffering through elective dental surgery rather than a happy family dinner to celebrate Marie's arrival.

"I could very easily not have invited you," Amelia said now. Pointedly. She sat on the settee in the dressing room of the guest suite where her mother had been installed, literal miles away from where she and Teo were. "If I thought you would come here and say snide things about fairy tales, I wouldn't have."

"You would have invited me no matter what," Marie said, with that laugh of hers, and that she was right only made Amelia scowl. "I'm your mother. We're stuck with each other no matter what."

"You're reminding me why I prefer to be stuck with you from a distance."

Marie had been attending to her toilette, but she turned around then, meeting Amelia's gaze straight on instead of through the mirror. And Amelia knew it wasn't what she'd just said, because such things rolled right off her deceptively steely mother.

"Are you sure you know what you're doing?" Marie asked instead.

"I'm getting married in two days," Amelia replied lightly. "It seems pretty straightforward. White dress, aisle, husband."

Her mother's smile was sad. "And then you're a duchess."

"There have been a great many duchesses. *Most* of them lived long enough to die of old age. Or what passed for old age in their time." She shrugged. "Again, perfectly straightforward."

"There's nothing straightforward about the de Luz family." Marie rolled her eyes, seeming to take in the whole of this impossible house, from all the treasures it held to the pedigree that seemed to ooze from its very walls. "You cannot simply marry the Duke. You must marry the dukedom, too. And everything that goes with it."

Amelia didn't like the way Marie was looking at her. "I thought you enjoyed endless wealth, social standing, cachet, whatever you want to call it."

"I do indeed." Her mother's gaze was kind, then, Amelia realized, but no less sad. Something inside her seemed to clutch at her heart, then hold it with too-tight claws. "But you do not care one way or another for any of those things. And if I found the Marinceli name too heavy a burden to bear, I wonder, what will it do to you?"

Her throat was dry, indicating a panic Amelia refused to entertain. "That hardly matters. I'm carrying his baby."

Marie made a small sighing sound. "Yes, yes. I'm sure he thundered on impressively about bloodlines that predate Spain, but so what? You can raise a child on your own, love. Whether Teo de Luz gives you permission or not."

"I don't know that I have it in me to deny my child a father when he's on offer, actually."

"You didn't miss having a father around," Marie said dismissively. "In fact, I think you thrived without one."

"That's a lovely story, Mom," Amelia said. Maybe with a little more heat than she'd intended, because that was bypassing all kinds of hurtful things that they pretended they'd settled years ago. Like the fact that Marie hadn't encouraged Amelia's relationship with her father while he was alive. And hadn't thought to save any keepsakes, either, since Amelia could barely remember a man she'd barely seen who'd died when she was five. It was one more reason she'd been determined to tell Teo about his child, so that part of history need not repeat itself. Not by her hand. "But it's your story. Not mine. I didn't have *my* father, but that didn't mean there weren't all kinds of father figures around. Most of them terrible."

"Most men are terrible. That's the tragedy of loving them." And if Amelia had thought that she could shame her mother, she was disappointed. Marie smiled, as merrily as ever. "And that's what I'm trying to tell you. You've had a thing about Teo forever."

"What? I haven't had a *thing*—"

"What I thought would save you is that he really, truly hates me and everything I touch," Marie continued as if Amelia hadn't protested. Or gone a shocking shade of red. "On the other hand, look at you."

Amelia didn't want to look at her reflection, because she didn't want to see herself turning into her mother. Right here in real time. Or maybe she wasn't turning into Marie fast enough. "I know what I look like."

"Fair enough," Marie said airily. But then her expression grew solemn again. "But Amelia, marrying the Duke of Marinceli is something that sounds good on paper. When really, it's a cage. I couldn't see myself in that cage. Are you sure you can?"

Amelia changed the subject, and Marie let her, but she couldn't get her mother's words out of her head as easily.

Later that afternoon, as the winter sun brooded its way into a gloomy evening, she made her way back to that study where she'd found Teo on her first day here. There was something about walking down that same hallway that got to her. She almost wanted to go fetch the butler and have him march with her, so she could fully reexperience it.

Then again, she already knew how it ended.

Amelia pushed open the door silently, and stood there a moment, watching Teo at work.

And she knew him now, in a way she never would have imagined was possible back when all she'd had of him was that *thing* her mother had clearly known about all the while. She knew what his close-cropped black hair felt like beneath her palms. She knew that his jaw would feel rough at this time of day, an erotic abrasion against her skin. She knew how he slept, which seemed an improbable miracle. What his face looked like in repose. She'd tasted him, everywhere. She'd felt those beautiful, aristocratic hands on every part of her body.

And yet as she looked at him, sitting at his desk going through stacks of documents his business manager would have left him earlier in the day, Amelia thought that she had never in her life seen a man so alone.

That wasn't something that seemed to change, no matter how well they seemed to know each other in bed. No matter how they talked, late at night, when the dark held him close and it seemed so much easier to share things that might make her blush in the light of day.

He told her secrets, there in the dark. His big hand on the back of her head she lay against his chest, his voice a rumble she could hear as well as feel beneath her. He told her what it was like to grow up knowing all of this would be his one day. She couldn't really remember her father, so he'd told her about his mother. She made him laugh. He made her heart swell.

It was those nights, laced together, that gave her hope. Or the mornings he would wake her, his hands spread over her growing belly, and that curve in the corner of his stern mouth as he talked in a low voice to their baby.

She thought they were getting somewhere. She really did. But her mother's words pounded her head tonight. They felt like a prophecy. Like a curse.

"I want more than a marriage of convenience," she blurted out.

And when Teo raised that simmering black gaze of his to hers, she understood that he'd known she was there all along. Had known it from the moment she'd turned down this particular hallway, if she had to guess.

"What do you propose instead?" he asked, and he still sounded austere. As affronted as he had the day she'd come here to tell him she was pregnant, but she could hear the laziness beneath it tonight. That casual hint of a drawl that she was sure was only hers.

"I want everything."

The ducal brow rose. "If there is more to everything than a lifetime as a Marinceli Duchess, I must confess I do not know what it is." He sat back in his chair, regarding her with that steadiness of his that was in itself reproving. "Is there something you want that you feel you cannot have? I find that hard to believe, Amelia. Look around. I am fairly certain I have everything. This means you do, too."

And she understood, as little as she wanted to, what her mother was trying to tell her.

It was easy to roll around in a bed. To let sex cloud her head and make her think it was the same as love. When it was only a part of it. An expression of it, certainly, but not the whole.

She slipped her hands over her belly and held them there, taking strength from the child she carried. Their child. The Twentieth Duke of this magical, monstrous place, and it was up to her to see to it that he was more than just a collection of musty old titles. That he was vivid and vulnerable, able to love and live. She didn't want for him the kind of life that her mother had given her, that Marie would call a madcap adventure and Amelia considered far more of a collection of catastrophes.

But Teo was a result of his childhood, too. And a father who had made certain Teo knew his duty, then left him to it.

There had to be a place between the two. *There had to be.*

And Amelia could think of only one way to achieve it.

"You have everything that money can buy," she said softly. "Ancient money. Modern money. And everything in between. If it can be claimed by might or money, you have it. I know that."

His brow rose even higher. "You are welcome, *cariña*."

"I want more," she said simply. Terribly. "I want love."

And she expected the very walls to crumble, perhaps. Or Teo to burst into flame. Something suitably dramatic for a man she was fairly certain had never experienced much love at all. Not in so many words.

"Love," he repeated, looking as if she'd suggested he fly naked over the whole of Spain. "I beg your pardon. Is it the wedding that is addling your senses, Amelia? What has love to do with anything?"

"Love has to do with everything," she said, and if it wasn't so important she might have been embarrassed by her own earnestness. "My mother gave me none of the security you take for granted, but she loved me. And you can argue *how much* all you like. You can claim she loves herself more. I know she does. I don't want to know it, but I do. And I may have spent too much of my life trying to get her to love me that much, too, but in the end, she still loves me just as much as she's able. What else is there?"

"This feels like a very Californian conversation," Teo said, distinct acid in his voice and his gaze dark. "Does it require my participation?"

There was nothing in that that should have emboldened her, but Amelia moved farther into the room, walking over to that massive desk of his and slapping her palms down on the surface—mostly to keep herself from reaching out to him.

"You can make fun all you like. But we're bringing a child into this world, and life is hard enough—even as a de Luz—without whatever version of tough love it is that your father gave you."

The ice Teo wore like armor cracked a little, then. She could see it in his eyes. And the tightness of his jaw. "My father raised me to step confidently into my position as Duke. A man is not a man unless he teaches his son how to take his place, and do better than he ever could."

"Then do better," Amelia challenged him. "What would happen if you not only trained your son to take your place, but taught him how to love? Openly. Fully. Not hidden behind talk of duties and bloodlines. What would happen then, Teo?"

"I don't understand any part of this conversation. We already made a deal. The wedding is in two days. Or is this some kind of a threat?"

Amelia made herself take a breath. She straightened from the desk, but still stood there, staring across at him. And he looked like some kind of a god. Haughty, untouchable. But it occurred to her for the first time that that thread of arrogance she saw in his expression was as much of a mask as the one she'd worn to the Masquerade.

*The Duke* was a costume.

The truth about this man was the dark. The weight of his hand on the nape of her neck. The stark need on his face as he drove inside her.

This urbane performance, this role, was the character he played.

She knew this as surely as she knew how much she already loved the son inside her. It was a simple fact made entirely of complexities and *what-ifs* and ferocity.

"I was a virgin," she said, suddenly flooded with a sense of calm. A purpose, even.

Teo laughed. "Do you mean, you were once a virgin? So were we all, Amelia."

"The night of the Masquerade," she said, and watched as he reacted to that. Badly. "That was the trouble, you see. I could never get past a kiss with another man. You were always in my head. It was as if I locked myself away when I left here as a teenager. And you were the only key."

"This is absurd."

"I thought so, too," she agreed. "That's why I went to such lengths last fall. I didn't want you to know who I was because I didn't want to explain this to you. I just wanted to do it, if it could be done."

"How could you have been a virgin?" he demanded, and he sounded almost...anguished.

And suddenly he was on his feet, separated from her only by the wide expanse of his desk.

"I think the usual way is by not having sex."

"That is not what I mean." To her astonishment, she saw Teo's hands curl into fists at his sides. "I mean you. How could *you* have been a virgin then?"

Understanding dawned, a bit like a kick to the solar plexus. It was possible she wheezed.

"Because, of course, you think my mother

is a whore." She shook her head, but it didn't help. "And it must be catching. Is that it?"

"I don't know what game this is you're trying to play," Teo threw at her, his voice low and hard in a way she'd never heard before. "And I don't know what you want out of this. Of me. Is it not enough that I am making you my wife? My Duchess? That because of that night, you have everything any reasonable person could possibly want or need? I don't understand the point of twisting it all around."

"It's not twisted," Amelia managed to say, though her lips were numb. "It's the truth. No more and no less."

"Enough of this, Amelia. It helps no one."

"Why does my innocence that night upset you?" she asked, but for all that odd calm inside her, there was a sadness, too.

Because she knew.

Teo said nothing. He only stared at her, and the stark expression on his face made her want to weep.

"It's so much easier if I'm simply the villain, isn't it?" she asked softly. "It makes so much more sense if I'm the Mata Hari in this story, who had my wicked way with you. You already know how to play the role of the victim, don't you?"

"How dare you call *me* the one playing victim."

But she ignored him. "What we know about you, Teo, is that you dearly love a role to play. Your father loved my mother too much and foisted her upon you. How could you do anything but hate her? And then there's me. My mother's daughter. Wouldn't it make everything perfect if I was a whore just like her?"

"Stop calling yourself a whore," he gritted out. "I have never used that word."

"You don't have to when it's written all over you."

"Amelia—" he started, but she didn't let him finish.

Not now. Not when she was this close to being fully and madly and foolishly honest with him. About everything, at last.

Because she didn't know any other way forward.

"Do you know why I did it?" she asked him, one hand on her belly. And not caring at all if he could see her emotions right there on her face. "Why I went to such lengths to give my virginity to a man who I knew wouldn't take it if it was offered? A man who I had to hide it from, hide my face from, hide *me* from?"

"I shudder to think."

She shook her head, sadly. And for a moment, she wondered if she really did dare to push this as far as it could go.

But she could feel the swell of her son beneath her palm. And she didn't know if it was possible to truly have everything. All of the Marinceli wealth and power *and* love? Could anyone really have all of that?

*If anyone can, it will be you,* she promised their baby. Fiercely.

And it had to start here. With her.

And with Teo.

"I think you already know," she said, letting out a sound that was like a laugh, but far too hollow. But she pushed away the fear, pressed her hand against her belly and held Teo's gaze with hers. Unflinchingly, so there could be no mistake. "I love you."

# CHAPTER ELEVEN

TEO WAS FROZEN SOLID, yet ash straight through. Charred, somehow, and the longer Amelia stood here dropping these bombs of hers, the less likely it seemed that he would ever recover.

"You do not love me," he told her, hardly recognizing his own voice. "Love is no part of this."

"Then how do you plan to be a father?" she replied.

Far too calmly, to his way of thinking.

"My father—"

"Your father, as far as anyone can tell, loved one person, Teo. You told me so yourself." And her hands were on her belly, making it impossible for him to look away. Making it impossible for him to think. "Is that what you want for this child?"

He had the sense that the walls around him

were crumbling, when he could see full well that was not the case. Because it was never the case. This house, this dukedom, endured. As he would endure, whether he liked it or not.

He tried again. "The Dukes of Marinceli—"

"I care about the dukedom," Amelia said quietly, cutting him off as surely as if she'd wielded a machete. "Don't get me wrong, I do. Because you care so very much. Because it is so important to you, and you have dedicated your whole life to it. I care about it, Teo. But I care a great deal more about the man. About you."

"I did not ask for any of this." He heard the words come out of his mouth, and the strangest part was, he couldn't even bring himself to pull them back. To temper them. "I did not ask for your disguise. Your virginity. Or this child. But I'm fully prepared to do what must be done. That does not mean—"

"I don't believe you."

Something in him stuttered, then stopped. He was terribly afraid it was his heart. He waited for the storied shooting pains in his arm. To drop to the floor and be done with this conversation, at the very least.

But Amelia's gaze was steady. Not without pain, it hurt him to note, but she didn't waver. And he didn't understand how on the one hand, he wanted to do something utterly out of character, like make a run for it. While on the other, he wanted to give thanks that this fierce creature would be the mother to his son. To the next Duke.

His own mother had been elegant. Soft and sweet. He had missed her when she was gone. He missed her still. He sometimes thought he would go to his own grave never ready to forgive his father for moving on, so fast and so shamelessly. But he had never considered her *protective* in any way. She had not had that kind of fierceness in her. Rather, she was one more thing he needed to defend.

He had done his best, hadn't he? He had hated Marie French in and out of his father's life, and still. He had done what he could in the face of his father's betrayal of her.

"You don't believe me?" He heard the harshness of his voice, yet did nothing to fix it. "I'm not the one who has made a habit of lying, Amelia. By omission or otherwise."

"I'm not even sure I believe that." When he stared at her, she shrugged. "Did you really not recognize me, Teo? Are you truly that unobservant? A different hair color and a mask, and suddenly a person you've known for half your life is a stranger? Why do I find that difficult to imagine?"

How ash could turn into more ash, and grow colder, he could not fathom. "I don't know what you're suggesting."

"And then, I turn up here out of the blue, and you let me in." Her head tilted slightly to one side, though that steady gaze didn't waver. "Which makes more sense, do you think? That you admitted the daughter of a woman you profess to hate without question and even claimed at first you couldn't remember her? Or that you admitted a lover who you'd seen quite intimately only a few months before?"

Teo was moving before he knew it. But not toward her. He rounded the desk and headed for his door before these things she was saying took root in him. And grew.

"These conspiracy theories are fascinating, I grant you that," he said gruffly as he went. "But they only make me question what goes on in your head. And whether or not I will need to limit your influence on the child you carry."

"Threats, threats, threats," she murmured, as he remembered she had before. "You say you don't want me. That I'm beneath you in every way. But it seems to me, Your Excellency, that the only way you're really interested in seeing me beneath you is in bed. And getting me there was the entire crux of your argument in that cabin. It wasn't that you need me to marry you. It was that you insisted on the marital bed."

Teo had stopped, there on the carpet where she had once stood and he'd imagined that she might know her place. But did he know his? Because the walls of this house might not have been crumbling. But he was.

He was already ash. He was quickly becoming little more than dirt, fit for little but a return to the earth. The land outside these walls that his ancestors had fought and died for.

What would he fight for? And if he didn't know the answer to that, how could he know what he would die for?

"I don't believe you," she said again.

And some other, terrible fury rose in him then. Suddenly, instead of making for the door, he advanced on her instead. But this was Amelia, so she did not shrink away. Her hands found her hips, her chin tilted up and she paid him exactly none of the deference that he was due. That he was given by every other person on this earth.

It was like a panic in him. Instead of finding it the greatest insult of all time, all Teo wanted was to get his hands on her.

Again. More. Always.

He did.

He gripped her shoulders in his palms, and he didn't know which one of them he was punishing when he didn't pull her close to get his mouth on her.

"I do not know what this is," he said as sternly as he could, as if he could hide the way he was crumbling inside. "But it's too late. Nothing you say to me, nothing you use to goad me with, will change the course of events. You will marry me."

"You're damn right I'm going to marry you," she shot back. "Here's a newsflash for you, Teo. I'm not my mother. I've loved one man, ever. And I have every intention of loving you for the rest of my life."

"I cannot help you in such a futile endeavor."

"And you will love me back," she told him, again with that steady, demanding gaze. "Believe me. You will. I won't accept anything else."

"You will accept what you are given," he told her, furiously. "Which in your case, is a great deal indeed."

"The truth is," she said softly, "I'm halfway to believing you already love me."

His hands tightened on her shoulders, and her lips parted, and he could feel that awareness that was always between them sizzle. He knew what it meant. It would be so easy to follow it. To shift this conversation onto ground he understood.

Instead, he released her.

Though it cost him.

"I cannot love you," he told her, stiff and formal, every inch of him the Duke of Marinceli he'd been trained to become. Handing down his word as law. "I'm not capable of it, don't you understand? Nor do I wish to become capable of it. That is not who I am."

Her eyes were still too wide, that impossible violet, and he had the terrible sensation that she could see everything. As if he was transparent.

"It is exactly who you are," she said, fervently. "I'll show you."

"Like hell you will," he threw at her. "I am the Duke of Marinceli, Amelia. This is not a coffee date with credit card debt to look forward to. This is an ancient dukedom and *that* is the prize. *That* is what you get. I would strongly suggest you work on gratitude, but if you do not, there is no need to worry. There is a reason the estate is as big as it is." When she stared back at him without comprehension, his lips twisted. "There are ample alternative residences on the property to stash a duchess who has given herself over to bitterness. You should have paid more attention to the history books while you were here as a teenager."

And then, before he lost control of himself completely and did something he couldn't take back—like surrender to the emotions racking him that he wasn't sure he even believed were real—Teo made himself walk away.

That night, for the first time since she'd come into his bedroom in the cabin, Teo did not share a bed with Amelia. Or touch her at all. He avoided the dinner he knew she was having with her mother, and lost himself instead in estate matters he could easily have put off if he'd wished.

He did not wish.

And another cold winter's morning was

dawning when he found himself wandering the halls of this place he knew too well, as if all the history his ancestors had lived out here had sunk into the floorboards. As if it could infuse him with the lessons they'd learned. Or not learned.

Teo found himself in the gallery, staring at portraits of the nineteen men who had come before him. Some who had fought wars to keep this land and this house in the family. Others who had fought their own inclinations, grasping kings and queens, and their own baser instincts.

He stood for a long time in front of the portrait of his own father.

Until yesterday, he would have said he knew his father at least as well as he knew this house, these lands. Strengths and weaknesses alike.

Now he felt he didn't know anything at all. Least of all himself.

He braced himself when he heard a soft sound behind him, a footfall, expecting it to be Amelia.

But it was worse. It was her mother.

"Jet lag," she said, smiling at him with too much familiarity. "I've been up since three o'clock."

"My condolences, madam," Teo said in as frosty a tone as he could manage.

"Only you can make that word sound like an insult. *Madam.*" She let out that bawdy, problematic laugh of hers that had bothered Teo for over a decade. "Marie will do just fine, thank you."

Teo had no intention of spending enough time talking to this woman that it would matter what he called her. He inclined his head stiffly, then made to go.

"I know you think I broke his heart," Marie said, shocking Teo into standing still. "It was the other way around."

Teo decided he'd had enough of up being down. Inside being out.

Then and there.

"Is that what you call it?" he asked tightly, glaring at her. "Heartbreak? I've heard other terms used to describe what you do, *Marie.*"

If his tone ruffled her feathers, she didn't show it. "Your father was exciting. Inventive in a variety of ways, though I don't expect that's something you'd like to hear any more about."

It took Teo a moment to understand her meaning. Then he was appalled. "I cannot think of anything I would like to know less."

"But he didn't love me," Marie said, very simply and distinctly. And there was something about the way she was looking at him. That clever face of hers that he saw too much of Amelia in, washed with something he was very much afraid was sadness. Real sadness. "Your father loved one thing and one thing only."

"It wasn't my mother," Teo retorted. "If you mean the dukedom, that was his duty."

Marie smiled, but that didn't wipe away the sadness. "He cared for your mother, in his way. And he took the dukedom very seriously. But what your father truly loved was getting his way. That wasn't a broken heart you saw when we were done. It was a temper tantrum."

Teo shook his head, refusing to take her words on board. "You ruined him. He lost himself in a bender of scandalous women and—"

Marie reached over and tapped her finger against the ornate frame that held Luis Calvo's portrait in place.

"Come now, Teo," she said quietly. "When do you recall your father truly losing it? Ever?" She actually laughed at Teo's expression, then. "It was his way or the highway.

Always. I chose the highway. And here's my advice to you, jet-lagged though it might be at this hour. You need to choose, Teo. Because a little-known truth in this world is that you usually have to choose between being right, or being happy."

His heart was pounding again, but still he didn't fall. "I don't know what that means."

"I have faith in you. You'll figure it out. And if you break my little girl's heart the way I think you will?" This time, Marie French's famous gaze was as steady as her daughter's, and far colder. "I'll actually do to you what you think I did to your father. Public shame is a game I play entirely too well."

Then she sauntered off and left him there, staring at the portrait of a man he could no longer recognize at all.

And if he didn't know his own father… If he didn't know the blood in his own veins when he had spent his life immersed in his own bloodline and what it meant and what it made him, then… Who was he?

Teo couldn't seem to move, as if he'd already been committed to stone, made a statue and had been left here in this gallery to take his place with all the other ciphers who gazed back at him from the walls.

If he didn't know who he was, how could he know who they had been? He'd studied their stories, taking notes on how best to be the Duke—but what kind of men were they? Had they loved anyone at all? Or were they all the same as his father? Powerful men who wanted their way above all things?

He couldn't dispute what Marie had said, though he'd wanted to. His father had liked his own way. And had always gotten it, running roughshod over anyone who came near him, including over Teo's mother—until he'd met Marie.

How had Teo managed to forget that?

Teo thought of his own behavior since Amelia had turned up here, pregnant with his child. Something he'd acted as if she had done herself when he could remember what had happened between them in vivid detail all these months later.

He had abducted her, taken her away and kept her there—treating her like a servant, which she had taken to alarmingly well but certainly didn't excuse him—until she'd agreed to come to his bed. He might as well be that warlord Duke from the early centuries, who had sacked whole cities in his zest to preserve his title.

Teo did not doubt that he could handle the dukedom. He'd been training for it his entire life.

But what kind of husband was he going to be? What kind of father? He wanted Amelia the way he'd had her in the cabin. The way he'd had her here, when they were alone. All that heat, intimate and raw.

And he wanted to be a better father than his own had been. He wanted to actually *be* a father—something more than a distant figure handing down pronouncements. Teo had no idea what that would look like, or what it would take, but he thought of that bump he liked to whisper to in the mornings and he wanted it. He wanted everything.

What was he willing to give it in return?

Amelia had offered him honesty. She had taken everything he'd thrown at her and handled it with an easy grace that humbled him. She'd come to him with soot on her face, thrown herself into his arms and dared him not to love her.

And that, right there, threatened to unman him entirely.

*Love.*

That was not what he would have called it, that night last fall. When he'd had his hands in her soft heat. When he'd taken her with such stark ferocity in that salon. She'd braced herself above him, and he'd held her there as she'd slowly impaled herself on him.

And he'd known her.

He'd denied it later, he'd called it a trick of the drink, but he'd known her.

Something on her face had changed as he'd lodged himself deep inside her, and a mask and red lipstick couldn't hide it.

Her name had scraped through his mind like a whisper. Like a curse.

After she'd left, he'd told himself that it hadn't happened. That he'd been mistaken.

And when she'd reappeared at his door, he'd told himself it was a coincidence. Even when she'd told him her news and confirmed what he'd already known, it had been easier to lose himself in the fury of her deception than it was to face the facts.

That he'd known. He'd suspected he knew who she was and he'd gone right ahead and done it anyway. As he'd sworn he wouldn't do.

And far more stunning than his own self-deception was the fact that she knew it. She knew all of it. The lies he told himself, the lies he told her. And still she said she loved him.

Teo felt those walls inside him crumble all the more.

He stood here in this gallery, surrounded by the stern faces of the men who made up this bloodline he was sworn to protect. And would, to his dying day.

But God help him, he wanted to be a better man while he did it.

He wanted to be the man Amelia loved. *All her life.* That's what she had said.

And this house couldn't help him. This glorious mausoleum to a highly curated past. He looked around this gallery at all those dark eyes so much like his and knew they couldn't help him. These men knew how to hold things in tight fists, not how to open themselves up.

Nothing here could help him.

But Teo thought he knew what would.

# CHAPTER TWELVE

THE NIGHT BEFORE the wedding was scheduled to take place, Amelia was giving herself a stern talking-to in the master suite that Teo had not entered since their confrontation in his study.

She wanted to rage about and throw things, the way her mother often did. But she wasn't her mother. And much as she imagined it must be satisfying to shatter something, the truth was… She just missed Teo.

That was the problem. And this time, she doubted very much that red hair dye and a mask would do the trick.

She was contemplating an heirloom vase, thick with flowers, that would make a lovely mess when tossed against the ancient wall when she heard the clearing of a throat from behind her.

Amelia turned to find the butler there,

staring back at her in that way of his that managed to be both condescending and obsequious at once. Now that she was going to be the Duchess of Marinceli in the morning, there was significantly more of the latter than the former. She was sorry that in her current state, she couldn't even enjoy it.

Because it was one thing to throw in Teo's face that she loved him, and would marry him as planned and continue to love him, and that she didn't much care what his take on that was.

It was something else again to…do it. To psych herself up for that walk down an aisle in an old chapel toward a man who claimed he could not love her. For the life that came after that walk, locked away in the timeless splendor of this place, like one more pretty object cluttering up the vast house.

For the family she would create with him, one way or another, and would have to do whether he loved her—or their son—or not.

It was the *or not* part that was sloshing around inside her tonight, making her feel as nauseated as she had throughout her first trimester.

"Your presence is requested, madam," the butler intoned, with excruciating courtesy.

Amelia didn't really want to go anywhere. Or do anything but sit where she was, and perhaps break some crockery. The wedding in the morning was private, mostly so that Teo could manipulate the timeline later to suit his purposes. A quiet announcement in five months' time to cover both the wedding and the birth of his heir, Teo had said.

Because the Duke of Marinceli did not explain himself to anyone. Much less perform for the masses. He was a de Luz, not a Windsor.

But, of course, a private wedding meant that her friends wouldn't be there. The people she loved, who loved her, unreservedly. In theory, she understood why it had to be this way. In her heart, she knew her friends would understand, *because* they loved her unreservedly. And she knew with every part of her, heart and soul and body, that she loved Teo enough that it would all be worth it.

There was tonight to get through, that was all. A little dark night of the soul before a lovely morning after. Teo thought he couldn't love anyone, least of all her, and she might have decided to ignore that—but that didn't mean it didn't hurt.

Amelia, by God, would be a little blue if she felt like it.

But she got up and followed the butler anyway, because there was a point at which *a little blue* became full-on wallowing, and she was pretty sure she'd already passed it some ways back. And besides, she preferred her crockery intact.

The butler led her out through the house, processing in all his state down one meandering hallway to another. He took her out the grand front entry and handed her into a waiting car, then presented her with her coat with theatrical flourish.

Amelia shrugged into her coat as the car slid away from the front of the house. When the driver turned deeper into the property instead of down the drive, Amelia felt a little prickle of foreboding. Or premonition, anyway. Sure enough, the car delivered her to the waiting private jet out on the estate's airfield.

And there seemed to be nothing to do but board it. Amelia climbed up the steps as the winter wind picked up around her, playing with her hair and sending icy fingers creeping down beneath the collar of her trusty peacoat.

Inside, she expected to find Teo lounging

about, looking like royalty. But the jet was empty, save for the staff. She even checked the staterooms, but no. She had the sleek aircraft to herself.

And when the plane landed sometime later in that same remote airfield high in the Pyrenees that she knew all too well, Amelia had worked herself into a full-on temper.

"The Duke is waiting for you, madam," the captain told her when he emerged from the cockpit. He gestured deferentially toward the door.

Amelia considered refusing to leave the plane. But she had the feeling that wouldn't go quite as she wanted it to. She imagined Teo would have no problem whatsoever storming onto the plane and collecting her, if he had a mind to. And she was in a righteous temper, thank you, and didn't want him *collecting* her like a recalcitrant child.

She made herself get up. She stepped outside, gasping involuntarily at the slap of the cold, complete with dancing snow flurries. Something she found markedly prettier when she was indoors, preferably next to a crackling fire with something warm to drink. But the weather wasn't the only thing that stole her breath.

At the bottom of the jetway steps, Teo waited.

Seemingly impervious to the weather.

Amelia forced herself to take a breath. She thought uncharitable things about the humanity of the average duke. And then she stormed down the metal stairs until she reached him.

"You must have truly lost your mind if you think that I'm going to play this Cinderella game with you again," she threw at him, not caring if the captain was watching them. Not caring if he heard every word she said. "Cinderella only works when you know how it ends. The point isn't the toiling away at all that menial labor. It's when the charming prince rescues her and sweeps her away from all that. Prince Charming, Teo. Not…you."

That muscle moved in his cheek, broadcasting his own temper. But he didn't say a word. He only beckoned her to the SUV parked to the side of the runway with its engine running. He opened the door for her to get in, then waited. Watching her.

Daring her.

"I'm not kidding, Teo," Amelia said crossly. "I will not—"

"Do you wish to argue with me here?" he asked in that silky, dangerous way of his that still did things to her she would've preferred not to acknowledge. "I am personally not interested in hypothermia in such a remote place, *cariña*. I cannot imagine it will suit our son. But for you, I will risk it."

Wordlessly, furiously, she climbed into his SUV.

And even though she was prepared for it this time, the winding road still got to her. Around and around and around, lurching this way and that as he headed for the top of the mountain and the cabin that waited for them there.

Finally, they reached the summit, and Teo drove straight to the cabin door as he had the last time. The memories Amelia had of this cabin were fond, so it made something in her ache to see it again now, when she was so much less certain about where they were headed than she had been when they'd left here.

She added that to the fire inside her that was keeping her temper humming along nicely.

It was much snowier and much windier this high up. Amelia hunched her shoulders deeper into her coat as she got out, picking her way across the snowy yard to the heavy front door. She wasn't dressed for this weather. The shoes she wore were better suited to a San Francisco winter, which was often wet and cold, but was certainly not a mountaintop blizzard, for God's sake.

She was already simmering with fury about the fire he would make her build. The orders he would bark at her and the demands he would make. But this time, she had no intention of doing a thing. Not one thing. He could—

But what he did was swing open the door, and her breath—and temper—went out of her in a rush.

Because the fire was already built and crackling along nicely, heating up the cabin. The lanterns were lit. It was homey, bright.

It made her throat feel thick. Tight.

Amelia moved inside on legs that felt suddenly jerky and strange, and felt the jolt of it when he closed the door behind them.

"Did you bring your own maid this time?" she asked, and much as she might have wanted to pretend that she kept the bitterness from her voice, she could hear it herself.

"Only if you consider me a maid," came Teo's cool, amused voice. "And I must tell you, *cariña*, I do not."

He moved past her, farther into the room. Toward those couches that loomed large in her head. She'd slept on one of those couches, in what she could see, now, had been an extended act of defiance. Because, against her will—and though she'd been so sure she'd exorcised him from her life, no matter that she carried his child—she had fallen in love with him. When she was sixteen. Again last fall.

And most certainly—permanently and irrevocably—here.

"I don't understand why you brought me back here," she managed to say, miserably. "Especially with all that snow out there. What if we're trapped here? Have you forgotten that we're to be married in the morning?"

"Are you afraid of being stuck here, Amelia?"

She was. She scowled at him. "It's more accurate to say I would prefer not to be stuck anywhere."

"It is our wedding, *cariña*," he replied, and though his voice was soft, his expression was all stone and strength. "If we're not there, they will simply have to wait until we are."

He was over by the couches now, standing there as if he expected her to come and join him. But Amelia didn't want to move from the door. She felt the same mess of things she always felt when it came to Teo. All tangled around each other, snarled and knotted and bent back on themselves. And it all grew inside her chest as she looked at him, and in her gut, like a terrible sob.

She understood that she would love him forever. She had accepted that. But she had wanted tonight—just tonight—to mourn what couldn't be. To prepare herself for a wedding to a man who had vowed he would never love her. She might not believe he was right about that, but her belief didn't make the reality any easier to bear.

But this was worse.

"I had hoped you might sit and talk to me awhile," Teo said when all she did was glare at him. "But you don't look as if you wish to step another foot inside this cabin."

"I don't know what you want from me." That sob was inside her, growing all the while, but she fought valiantly to keep it there. "If it's for me to act like a domestic servant the way I did before, you should know that I only ever took to that because it was temporary. And my choice. You can't really think you're going to haul me up here every time you need a floor mopped or a—"

"Amelia."

It was the way he said it. His voice seemed to ring in her, loud and long. As if her name was a song all its own and he alone knew how to sing it.

And then he was prowling back across the floor toward her, never shifting that black-gold gaze from her face.

"I do not want you to clean my floor," he said as he came closer. "I do not want you to do anything, unless you wish to do it."

She pulled in a breath, but when she went to speak... She couldn't.

Teo was before her. And then, while she watched—her heart in her throat and that sob so much of her that maybe it *was* her—he sank to his knees. Right there on the floor she'd once scrubbed on her hands and knees.

"What are you doing?" she whispered.

"I have already ordered you to marry me," Teo said, still holding her gaze, seeming unaware that if he was another man this might have been a humbling moment. But he looked proud. Certain. And he gazed only at her. "And you have graciously indicated that you would obey. Tonight I rather thought I would ask."

It was as if the world stood still. Or turned too fast. Amelia couldn't quite tell.

All she knew was that everything was different, impossible. And Teo, the Nineteenth Duke of Marinceli, was on his knees.

Gazing up at her as if she was the world, still or spinning or both.

And, while she watched—stunned—he reached into his pocket and pulled out a ring.

There were no fancy boxes, no ribbons. But this was the sort of ring that needed no extra ornamentation.

It looked like the kind of ring that wars were fought over. And given who was holding it, Amelia assumed that was a distinct possibility.

"This belonged to the Twelfth Duchess," Teo told her, holding the ring so the lantern light caught it and made it shine like a promise. "She had an eye for the finer things. But, more importantly, she is chiefly known for refusing the Twelfth Duke. Three times, or so the story goes. It was not until he took the time and trouble to abduct her, convince her and get her with child, that she condescended to accept his suit. Such as it was."

"She sounds like my kind of girl," Amelia managed to say, though her throat ached. And that sob she'd been trying to keep at bay had transferred too much heat to the back of her eyes. She was afraid that at any moment tears might tip over and betray her completely.

"The Twelfth Duke and his Duchess lived a very long time," Teo replied in that same steady, certain way. "Together. And if the stories are true, they loved each other very much."

He reached over then and took her hand in his, and Amelia stopped pretending that she could breathe through this.

"Amelia." And again, her name was like a song in his mouth. "I've spent my whole life training how to become not just any duke, but the Duke of Marinceli. To live up to all these stories, all these august men in this world they built and left to me to protect. There is nothing I do not know about my land, my house, my history. But I neglected to make certain that I was also becoming a decent man."

"Teo..." she tried to say.

"And I don't know if I can be anything approaching decent," he said as if she hadn't spoke, his voice rougher now. "I don't know if that's possible, after all these years spent ignoring that part of me. But I will tell you this. I want to be him, for you. A better man, whatever that looks like. Whatever it takes. Because you deserve nothing less."

And the tears fell then, but Amelia did nothing to wipe them away. She let them fall.

As if this was a kind of baptism, hers and his alone.

"I knew it was you," he told her then, his gaze so intense it almost burned. But she didn't look away. She couldn't bear to look away. "At the Masquerade. Your name was in my head, and I dismissed it. I told myself I was mistaken. But it was there."

Amelia pulled one of her hands from his, and slid her palm along the hard line of his jaw. And then she held him there, this beautiful, powerful man, who seemed in no way diminished because he knelt before her.

On the contrary. He seemed raw. Sincere. More powerful than ever before.

And he made her heart thump hard and wild inside her.

"I don't know that my father truly loved anything but his own position," Teo said in that same quiet way that rang in her, through her, until her bones seemed a part of that same ringing. "I had to go back generations to find the Twelfth Duke and Duchess, because as I told you, de Luzes do not marry for love. Not usually. But Amelia, I want nothing more. I want to marry you. I want to have this baby and raise him with you, with love. And I say this as a man who has no idea if I'm even capable of these things."

"Of course you are," she said then, fiercely. "You are the Duke of Marinceli, aren't you? You're capable of anything. By definition."

"This is what I believe, with all that I am, Duke and man alike," Teo said then, his face in her hand and that glorious, ancient ring between them. "If you believe in me, if you have this faith in me, I can be and do anything at all."

And he held up the ring then, so it caught the dancing light from the lanterns. It was an impossibly large sapphire, ringed with perfect diamonds and scattered here and there with rubies. It didn't look like a ring so much as it looked like a coronation.

And yet when Teo slipped it on her finger, it slid into place. And fit so perfectly it made a different sort of sob well up in Amelia's chest.

"Amelia," he said with that same intensity. "Will you marry me? Will you become my Duchess in every possible way? Will you teach me how to be a better man, point out when I stray too far into my title and remind me I am a husband and a father first?"

And she couldn't believe this was happening. But there was the weight of that ring on her finger, and the shine of it, which paled into insignificance next to that brilliant gleam in his beautiful dark eyes.

"It would be my honor to love you forever," Amelia said solemnly. "I already have, Teo. I always will."

"I love you, Amelia," Teo said, and that raw look on his face almost brought her to her knees, too. "I am not sure I have ever loved anyone or anything else. I know I never will."

Then he smiled, and it was not that stern quirk of his austere lips.

Tonight, he smiled wide. Open.

And Amelia knew that this Teo was the better man he thought he needed help to become, not the Duke he already was and ever would be. And both of them were hers.

Forever.

"And I love you, too," Teo murmured, spreading his hands over the thick swell of her belly and leaning close to press his mouth there, too, as if to speak directly to the baby. *"Te adoro, hijo mío."*

And that time, Amelia really did sink down to her knees, so she could get close to him.

This man who had cast his shadow over the whole of her life, and only now, only here, had they turned that shadow into dancing light. The two of them, together.

"I love you, Teo," she whispered, his face between her hands and all that bright light gleaming like hope around them.

And it was right there, on the floor that she had scrubbed on her hands and knees, that they stripped each other of their last remaining inhibitions—along with all their inconvenient clothes—and pledged themselves to their future.

As long as it was together.

# CHAPTER THIRTEEN

IT SNOWED FOR DAYS, stranding them at the cabin and pushing back their wedding a full week.

Neither the bride nor the groom appeared to care.

Teo stood at the head of the small aisle in the medieval chapel tucked away in the Marinceli estate near one of its private lakes, and felt his heart crack wide open as Amelia walked toward him with that gorgeous smile on her face. And nothing but love and happiness in her violet eyes.

She promised to be his forever.

He made the same promise.

And intended to keep it, if he had to dismantle every last stone of *el monstruo* to do it.

He would use his own two hands. Cheerfully.

The months passed, and Amelia grew big.

Then bigger still. Then so truly enormous that she began to joke that she might need a golf cart to get around the sprawling house.

"It is beneath the dignity of the Duchess of Marinceli to zoom about the ancestral seat of the dukedom in a mechanized conveyance, *cariña*," Teo told her in that cool, stuffy voice he liked to use. Because it always made her laugh.

And he loved to make her laugh.

"As you wish, Your Excellency," she replied when her laughter faded, grinning at him. "I hope it is not beneath the dignity of the Duke of Marinceli, then, to cart me about from place to place upon command."

"It is a very height of dignity, in fact. It is also a privilege."

And then he showed her exactly how dignified he could be as he swept her into his arms, then carried her to their bed.

The much-anticipated, already beloved Twentieth Duke of Marinceli was born at home, in the guest suite that had been made over into a neonatal clinic for precisely this purpose. And the Twentieth Duke was not concerned with dignity. He was big, healthy and very, very loud.

"He's suitably arrogant already," Amelia

declared as they lay on the bed together with their perfect, beautiful son between them. She was smiling down at the baby, and Teo couldn't imagine how he'd gotten this lucky. "Can world domination be far behind?"

Teo laughed, overcome at the miraculous thing his wife had done. And at the tiny, shrunken, perfect creature with red fists and an unholy temper that was now his, too.

And he did not plan to raise another robot of a duke. He would raise a good man, first. And see to the dukedom afterward.

He swore it, there and then, on the bed where he and Amelia had brought a new life into the world—and this ancient house—and had become a family.

Over the years, he and Amelia did not always get along. They did not always see eye to eye. But they fought behind closed doors, so as not to inflict their turmoil on their children. And they made up behind those same closed doors, because whatever else they felt, and no matter how furious they were with each other, they always had that flame.

That beautiful need that had drawn them together, and kept them together.

And as the years passed, Teo and Amelia added considerably to the bloodline. But they called it their family. Three sons, two daughters, and Amelia always said she would stop when she grew tired.

So far, neither one of them was tired.

And when one or the other of them felt that tiredness coming on, or felt that things had gotten too distant between them, whether through intent or accident, they removed themselves from the dukedom. A weekend here, another ten days there, they went back to the cabin and reminded themselves who they were.

"I love you," he said on one such morning, stripped out before the fire with his violet-eyed love. "It seems impossible, but it grows and grows. I love you more now than I did before. I keep waiting for it to diminish, but it keeps expanding."

"That's the magic of fairy tales," she said, propping herself up on his chest and smiling down at him, the way she had in this very cabin so many years before. The way he hoped she always would, with precisely that smile, and that dancing light in her pretty eyes.

"I thought Cinderella was all toil, a spell and then a lot of carrying on with mice and a pumpkin."

"Yes, but that's not the most important part," Amelia said. Sternly, even.

And Teo looked over her smooth, naked shoulder to that door she had pushed open all those years before her, and opened herself up to him. That was the second gift he'd given her the night he proposed, like a man. Instead of the orders he'd given her as the Duke. Her sooty handprint had remained, so he had carved it into the door. Then blackened it. So it would always be there, reminding him that whole lives could change in an instant. All one had to do was reach out a hand.

"I thought the most important part was you," he said. "It is certainly the most important part to me."

"I love you, too," she said. Her smile widened. "You know how fairy tales end. It's happily ever after. Ever after, not, you know, a few years here and there, in a nasty divorce, and happy forever means that you have to keep falling in love. It's right there in the rules. It has to grow, or doesn't count."

"Funny, I've never heard this law before."

"Stick with me," she told him, her violet eyes sparkling. "I'm the Duchess of Marinceli. My word is law."

Her word was certainly his law, but as besotted as Teo might have been, he wasn't quite so foolish as to say so.

Instead, he rolled her over, and smiled down at her.

And then, together, they got to work on that ever-after.

\* \* \* \* \*

*If you fell in love with*
Secrets of His Forbidden Cinderella
*by Caitlin Crews*
*you're sure to adore these other*
*One Night With Consequences stories!*

His Cinderella's One-Night Heir
*by Lynne Graham*
The Sicilian's Surprise Love-Child
*by Carol Marinelli*
Bound by Their Nine-Month Scandal
*by Dani Collins*
The Queen's Baby Scandal
*by Maisey Yates*

*Available now*